The
Harlequin
Tea Set

and Other Stories

The Harlequin Tea Set

and Other Stories

Agatha Christie

Thorndike Press • Thorndike, Maine

This Large Print edition is published by Thorndike Press, USA and by Chivers Press, England.

The Harlequin Tea Set and Other Stories Published in 1998 in the U.S. by arrangement with G.P. Putnam's Sons, a member of Penguin Putnam Inc.

While the Light Lasts Published in 1998 in the U.K. by arrangement with HarperCollins Publishers.

U.S.	Hardcover	0-7862-1408-2	(Basic Series Edition)
U.K.	Hardcover	0-7540-1150-X	(Windsor Large Print)
U.K.	Softcover	0-7540-2107-6	(Paragon Large Print)

Foreword and Afterword to Agatha Christie's "Manx Gold" by Tony Medawar.

"The Actress" first appeared in *Novel* magazine, 1923, London. "The Edge" first appeared in *Pearson's* magazine, 1927, London. "The Lonely God" first appeared in *Royal* magazine, 1926, London. "Manx Gold" first appeared in *The Daily Dispatch*, 1930, London. "The House of Dreams" first appeared in *Sovereign* magazine, 1926, London. "While the Light Lasts" first appeared in *Novel* magazine, 1923, London. "Within a Wall" first appeared in *Royal* magazine, 1925, London. "The Mystery of the Spanish Chest" first appeared as "The Mystery of the Bagdad Chest" in *The Regatta Mystery and Other Stories*, Dodd, Mead, New York, 1939. "The Harlequin Tea Set" first appeared in *Winter's Crimes*, Macmillan UK, London, 1971.

The text of this Large Print edition is unabridged.
Other aspects of the book may vary from the original edition.

Set in 16 pt. Plantin by Juanita Macdonald.

Printed in the United States on permanent paper.

British Library Cataloguing in Publication Data available

Library of Congress Cataloging in Publication Data

Christie, Agatha, 1890–1976.
    The harlequin tea set and other stories / Agatha Christie.
        p.   cm.
    Contents: The edge — The actess — While the light lasts — Th FELD
of dreams — The lonely god — Manx gold — Within a wall — '
mystery of the Spanish chest — The harlequin tea set.
    ISBN 0-7862-1408-2 (lg. print : hc : alk. paper)
    1. Detective and mystery stories, English. 2. Large type books.
[PR6005.H66H34   1998]
823'.912—dc21   9£

04/28/9

Contents

I

The Edge

Clare Halliwell walked down the short path that led from her cottage door to the gate. On her arm was a basket, and in the basket was a bottle of soup, some home-made jelly, and a few grapes. There were not many poor people in the small village of Daymer's End, but such as there were were assiduously looked after, and Clare was one of the most efficient of the parish workers.

Clare Halliwell was thirty-two. She had an upright carriage, a healthy color, and nice brown eyes. She was not beautiful, but she looked fresh and pleasant and very English. Everybody liked her and said she was a good sort. Since her mother's death, two years ago, she had lived alone in the cottage with her dog, Rover. She kept poultry and was fond of animals and of a healthy outdoor life.

As she unlatched the gate, a two-seater car swept past, and the driver, a girl in a red hat, waved a greeting. Clare responded, but for a moment her lips tightened. She felt that pang at her heart which always came when she saw Vivien Lee. Gerald's wife!

Medenham Grange, which lay just a mile outside the village, had belonged to the Lees for many generations. Sir Gerald Lee, the present owner of the Grange, was a man old for his years and considered by many stiff in manner. His pomposity really covered a good deal of shyness. He and Clare had played together as children. Later they had been friends, and a closer and dearer tie had been confidently expected by many — including, it may be said, Clare herself. There was no hurry, of course — but someday — She left it so in her own mind. Someday.

And then, just a year ago, the village had been startled by the news of Sir Gerald's marriage to a Miss Harper — a girl nobody had ever heard of!

The new Lady Lee had not been popular in the village. She took not the faintest interest in parochial matters, was bored by hunting, and loathed the country and outdoor sports. Many of the wiseacres shook their heads and wondered how it would end. It was easy to see where Sir Gerald's infatuation had come in. Vivien was a beauty. From head to foot she was a complete contrast to Clare Halliwell — small, elfin, dainty, with golden-red hair that curled enchantingly over her pretty ears, and big violet eyes that could shoot a sideways glance of provocation to the manner born.

Gerald Lee, in his simple man's way, had been anxious that his wife and Clare should be great friends. Clare was often asked to dine at the Grange, and Vivien made a pretty pretence of affectionate intimacy whenever they met. Hence that gay salutation of hers this morning.

Clare walked on and did her errand. The vicar was also visiting the old woman in question, and he and Clare walked a few yards together afterwards before their ways parted. They stood still for a minute discussing parish affairs.

"Jones has broken out again, I'm afraid," said the vicar. "And I had such hopes after he had volunteered, of his own accord, to take the pledge."

"Disgusting," said Clare crisply.

"It seems so to us," said Mr. Wilmot, "but we must remember that it is very hard to put ourselves in his place and realize his temptation. The desire for drink is unaccountable to us, but we all have our own temptations, and thus we can understand."

"I suppose we have," said Clare uncertainly.

The vicar glanced at her.

"Some of us have the good fortune to be

very little tempted," he said gently. "But even to those people their hour comes. Watch and pray, remember, that ye enter not into temptation."

Then bidding her good-bye, he walked briskly away. Clare went on thoughtfully, and presently she almost bumped into Sir Gerald Lee.

"Hullo, Clare. I was hoping to run across you. You look jolly fit. What a color you've got."

The color had not been there a minute before. Lee went on:

"As I say, I was hoping to run across you. Vivien's got to go off to Bournemouth for the weekend. Her mother's not well. Can you dine with us Tuesday instead of tonight?"

"Oh, yes! Tuesday will suit me just as well."

"That's all right, then. Splendid. I must hurry along."

Clare went home to find her one faithful domestic standing on the doorstep looking out for her.

"There you are, miss. Such a to-do. They've brought Rover home. He went off on his own this morning, and a car ran clean over him."

Clare hurried to the dog's side. She adored animals, and Rover was her especial darling.

She felt his legs one by one, and then ran her hands over his body. He groaned once or twice and licked her hand.

"If there's any serious injury, it's internal," she said at last. "No bones seem to be broken."

"Shall we get the vet to see him, miss?"

Clare shook her head. She had little faith in the local vet.

"We'll wait until tomorrow. He doesn't seem to be in great pain, and his gums are a good color, so there can't be much internal bleeding. Tomorrow, if I don't like the look of him, I'll take him over to Skippington in the car and let Reeves have a look at him. He's far and away the best man."

On the following day, Rover seemed weaker, and Clare duly carried out her project. The small town of Skippington was about forty miles away, a long run, but Reeves, the vet there, was celebrated for many miles around.

He diagnosed certain internal injuries but held out good hopes of recovery, and Clare went away quite content to leave Rover in his charge.

There was only one hotel of any pretensions in Skippington, the County Arms. It was mainly frequented by commercial travelers, for there was no good hunting country near Skippington, and it was off the track of the main roads for motorists.

Lunch was not served till one o'clock, and as it wanted a few minutes of that hour, Clare amused herself by glancing over the entries in the open visitors' book.

Suddenly she gave a stifled exclamation. Surely she knew that handwriting, with its loops and whirls and flourishes? She had always considered it unmistakable. Even now she could have sworn — but of course it was clearly impossible. Vivien Lee was at Bournemouth. The entry itself showed it to be impossible: *Mr. and Mrs. Cyril Brown, London.*

But in spite of herself her eyes strayed back again and again to that curly writing, and on an impulse she could not quite define she asked abruptly of the woman in the office:

"Mrs. Cyril Brown? I wonder if that is the same one I know?"

"A small lady? Reddish hair? Very pretty. She came in a red two-seater car, madam. A Peugeot, I believe."

Then it was! A coincidence would be too remarkable. As if in a dream, she heard the woman go on:

"They were here just over a month ago for a weekend, and liked it so much that they have come again. Newly married, I should fancy."

Clare heard herself saying: "Thank you. I don't think that could be my friend."

Her voice sounded different, as though it belonged to someone else. Presently she was sitting in the dining room, quietly eating cold roast beef, her mind a maze of conflicting thought and emotions.

She had no doubts whatever. She had summed Vivien up pretty correctly on their first meeting. Vivien was that kind. She wondered vaguely who the man was. Someone Vivien had known before her marriage? Very likely — it didn't matter — nothing mattered but Gerald.

What was she — Clare — to do about Gerald? He ought to know — surely he ought to know. It was clearly her duty to tell him. She had discovered Vivien's secret by accident, but she must lose no time in acquainting Gerald with the facts. She was Gerald's friend, not Vivien's.

But somehow or other she felt uncomfortable. Her conscience was not satisfied. On the face of it, her reasoning was good, but duty and inclination jumped suspiciously together. She admitted to herself that she disliked Vivien. Besides, if Gerald Lee were to divorce his wife — and Clare had no doubts at all that that was exactly what he would do, he was a man with an almost fanatical view of his own honor — then — well, the way would lie open for Gerald to come to her. Put like that, she shrank back fastidiously. Her own proposed action seemed naked and ugly.

The personal element entered in too much. She could not be sure of her own motives. Clare was essentially a high-minded, conscientious woman. She strove now very earnestly to see where her duty lay. She wished, as she had always wished, to do right. What was right in this case? What was wrong?

By a pure accident she had come into possession of facts that affected vitally the man she loved and the woman whom she disliked and — yes, one might as well be frank — of whom she was bitterly jealous. She could ruin that woman. Was she justified in doing so?

Clare had always held herself aloof from the back-biting and scandal which is an inevitable part of village life. She hated to feel that she now resembled one of those human ghouls she had always professed to despise.

Suddenly the vicar's words that morning flashed across her mind:

"Even to those people their hour comes."

Was this *her* hour? Was this *her* temptation? Had it come insidiously disguised as a duty? She was Clare Halliwell, a Christian, in love and charity with all men — and women. If she were to tell Gerald, she must be quite sure that only impersonal motives guided her. For the present she would say nothing.

She paid her bill for luncheon and drove away, feeling an indescribable lightening of spirit. Indeed, she felt happier than she had done for a long time. She felt glad that she had had the strength to resist temptation, to do nothing mean or unworthy. Just for a second it flashed across her mind that it might be a sense of power that had so lightened her spirits, but she dismissed the idea as fantastic.

By Tuesday night she was strengthened in her resolve. The revelation could not come through her. She must keep silence. Her own secret love for Gerald made speech impossible. Rather a high-minded view to take? Perhaps; but it was the only one possible for her.

She arrived at the Grange in her own little car. Sir Gerald's chauffeur was at the front door to drive it round to the garage after she had alighted, as the night was a wet one. He had just driven off when Clare remembered some books which she had borrowed and had brought with her to return. She called out, but the man did not hear her. The butler ran out after the car.

So, for a minute or two, Clare was alone in the hall, close to the door of the drawing room, which the butler had just unlatched prior to announcing her. Those inside the room, however, knew nothing of her arrival, and so it was that Vivien's voice, high-pitched — not quite the voice of a lady — rang out clearly and distinctly.

"Oh, we're only waiting for Clare Halliwell. You must know her — lives in the village — supposed to be one of the local belles, but frightfully unattractive really. She tried her best to catch Gerald, but he wasn't having any."

"Oh, yes, darling" — this in answer to a murmured protest from her husband. "She did — you mayn't be aware of the fact — but she did her very utmost. Poor old Clare! A good sort, but such a dump!"

Clare's face went dead white, her hands, hanging against her sides, clenched themselves in anger such as she had never known before. At that moment she could have murdered Vivien Lee. It was only by a supreme physical effort that she regained control of herself. That, and the half-formed thought that she held it in her power to punish Vivien for those cruel words.

The butler had returned with the books. He opened the door, announced her, and in another moment she was greeting a roomful of people in her usual pleasant manner.

Vivien, exquisitely dressed in some dark wine color that showed off her white fragility, was particularly affectionate and gushing. They didn't see half enough of Clare. She, Vivien, was going to learn golf, and Clare must come out with her on the links.

Gerald was very attentive and kind. Though he had no suspicion that she had overheard his wife's words, he had some vague idea of making up for them. He was very fond of Clare, and he wished Vivien wouldn't say the things she did. He and Clare had been friends, nothing more — and if there was an uneasy suspicion at the back of his mind that he was shirking the truth in that last statement, he put it away from him.

After dinner the talk fell on dogs, and Clare recounted Rover's accident. She purposely waited for a lull in the conversation to say:

17

"— so, on Saturday, I took him to Skip-pington."

She heard the sudden rattle of Vivien Lee's coffee cup on the saucer, but she did not look at her — yet.

"To see that man, Reeves?"

"Yes. He'll be all right, I think. I had lunch at the County Arms afterwards. Rather a decent little pub." She turned now to Vivien. "Have you ever stayed there?"

If she had had any doubts, they were swept aside. Vivien's answer came quick — in stammering haste.

"I? Oh! N-no, no."

Fear was in her eyes. They were wide and dark with it as they met Clare's. Clare's eyes told nothing. They were calm, scrutinizing. No one could have dreamed of the keen pleasure that they veiled. At that moment Clare almost forgave Vivien for the words she had overheard earlier in the evening. She tasted in that moment a fullness of power that almost made her head reel. She held Vivien Lee in the hollow of her hand.

The following day, she received a note from the other woman. Would Clare come up and have tea with her quietly that after-noon? Clare refused.

Then Vivien called on her. Twice she came at hours when Clare was almost certain to be at home. On the first occasion, Clare really was out; on the second, she slipped out by the back way when she saw Vivien coming up the path.

"She's not sure yet whether I know or not," she said to herself. "She wants to find out without committing herself. But she shan't — not until I'm ready."

Clare hardly knew herself what she was waiting for. She had decided to keep silence — that was the only straight and honorable course. She felt an additional glow of virtue when she remembered the extreme provocation she had received. After overhearing the way Vivien talked of her behind her back, a weaker character, she felt, might have abandoned her good resolutions.

She went twice to church on Sunday. First to early communion, from which she came out strengthened and uplifted. No personal feelings should weigh with her — nothing mean or petty. She went again to morning service. Mr. Wilmot preached on the famous prayer of the Pharisee. He sketched the life of that man, a good man, pillar of the church. And he pictured the slow, creeping blight of spiritual pride that distorted and soiled all that he was.

Clare did not listen very attentively. Vivien

was in the big square pew of the Lee family, and Clare knew by instinct that the other intended to get hold of her afterwards.

So it fell out. Vivien attached herself to Clare, walked home with her, and asked if she might come in. Clare, of course, assented. They sat in Clare's little sitting room, bright with flowers and old-fashioned chintzes. Vivien's talk was desultory and jerky.

"I was at Bournemouth, you know, last weekend," she remarked presently.

"Gerald told me so," said Clare.

They looked at each other. Vivien appeared almost plain today. Her face had a sharp, foxy look that robbed it of much of its charm.

"When you were at Skippington —" began Vivien.

"When I was at Skippington?" echoed Clare politely.

"You were speaking about some little hotel there."

"The County Arms. Yes. You didn't know it, you said?"

"I — I have been there once."

"Oh!"

She had only to keep still and wait. Vivien was quite unfitted to bear a strain of any kind. Already she was breaking down under

20

it. Suddenly she leaned forward and spoke vehemently.

"You don't like me. You never have. You've always hated me. You're enjoying yourself now, playing with me like a cat with a mouse. You're cruel — cruel. That's why I'm afraid of you, because deep down you're cruel."

"Really, Vivien!" said Clare sharply.

"You *know*, don't you? Yes, I can see that you know. You knew that night — when you spoke about Skippington. You've found out somehow. Well, I want to know what you are going to do about it. What are you going to do?"

Clare did not reply for a minute, and Vivien sprang to her feet.

"What are you going to do? I must know. You're not going to deny that you know all about it?"

"I do not propose to deny anything," said Clare coldly.

"You saw me there that day?"

"No. I saw your handwriting in the book — Mr. and Mrs. Cyril Brown."

Vivien flushed darkly.

"Since then," continued Clare quietly, "I have made inquiries. I find that you were not at Bournemouth that weekend. Your mother never sent for you. Exactly the same thing happened about six weeks previously."

Vivien sank down again on the sofa. She burst into furious crying, the crying of a frightened child.

"What are you going to do?" she gasped. "Are you going to tell Gerald?"

"I don't know yet," said Clare.

She felt calm, omnipotent.

Vivien sat up, pushing the red curls back from her forehead.

"Would you like to hear all about it?"

"It would be as well, I think."

Vivien poured out the whole story. There was no reticence in her. Cyril "Brown" was Cyril Haviland, a young engineer to whom she had previously been engaged. His health failed, and he lost his job, whereupon he made no bones about jilting the penniless Vivien and marrying a rich widow many years older than himself. Soon afterwards Vivien married Gerald Lee.

She had met Cyril again by chance. That was the first of many meetings. Cyril, backed by his wife's money, was prospering in his career, and becoming a well known figure. It was a sordid story, a story of backstairs meeting, of ceaseless lying and intrigue.

"I love him so," Vivien repeated again and again, with a sudden moan, and each time the words made Clare feel physically sick.

At last the stammering recital came to an end. Vivien muttered a shamefaced: "Well?"

"What am I going to do?" asked Clare. "I can't tell you. I must have time to think."

"You won't give me away to Gerald?"

"It may be my duty to do so."

"No, no." Vivien's voice rose to a hysterical shriek. "He'll divorce me. He won't listen to a word. He'll find out from that hotel, and Cyril will be dragged into it. And then his wife will divorce him. Everything will go — his career, his health — he'll be penniless again. He'd never forgive me — never."

"If you'll excuse my saying so," said Clare, "I don't think much of this Cyril of yours."

Vivien paid no attention.

"I tell you he'll hate me — hate me. I can't bear it. Don't tell Gerald. I'll do anything you like, but don't tell Gerald."

"I must have time to decide," said Clare gravely. "I can't promise anything offhand. In the meantime, you and Cyril mustn't meet again."

"No, no, we won't. I swear it."

"When I know what's the right thing to do," said Clare, "I'll let you know."

She got up. Vivien went out of the house in a furtive, slinking way, glancing back over her shoulder.

Clare wrinkled her nose in disgust. A beastly affair. Would Vivien keep her promise not to see Cyril? Probably not. She was weak — rotten all through.

That afternoon Clare went for a long walk. There was a path which led along the downs. On the left the green hills sloped gently down to the sea far below, while the path wound steadily upward. This walk was known locally as the Edge. Though safe enough if you kept to the path, it was dangerous to wander from it. Those insidious gentle slopes were dangerous. Clare had lost a dog there once. The animal had gone racing over the smooth grass, gaining momentum, had been unable to stop and had gone over the edge of the cliff to be dashed to pieces on the sharp rocks below.

The afternoon was clear and beautiful. From far below there came the ripple of the sea, a soothing murmur. Clare sat down on the short green turf and stared out over the blue water. She must face this thing clearly. What did she mean to do?

She thought of Vivien with a kind of disgust. How the girl had crumpled up, how abjectly she had surrendered! Clare felt a rising contempt. She had no pluck — no grit.

Nevertheless, much as she disliked Vivien,

Clare decided that she would continue to spare her for the present. When she got home she wrote a note to her, saying that although she could make no definite promise for the future, she had decided to keep silence for the present.

Life went on much the same in Daymer's End. It was noticed locally that Lady Lee was looking far from well. On the other hand, Clare Halliwell bloomed. Her eyes were brighter, she carried her head higher, and there was a new confidence and assurance in her manner. She and Lady Lee often met, and it was noticed on these occasions that the younger woman watched the older with a flattering attention to her slightest word.

Sometimes Miss Halliwell would make remarks that seemed a little ambiguous — not entirely relevant to the matter at hand. She would suddenly say that she had changed her mind about many things lately — that it was curious how a little thing might alter entirely one's point of view. One was apt to give way too much to pity — and that was really quite wrong.

When she said things of that kind she usually looked at Lady Lee in a peculiar way, and the latter would suddenly grow quite white, and look almost terrified.

But as the year drew on, these little subtleties became less apparent. Clare continued to make the same remarks, but Lady Lee seemed less affected by them. She began to recover her looks and spirits. Her old gay manner returned.

One morning, when she was taking her dog for a walk, Clare met Gerald in a lane. The latter's spaniel fraternized with Rover, while his master talked to Clare.

"Heard our news?" he said buoyantly. "I expect Vivien's told you."

"What sort of news? Vivien hasn't mentioned anything in particular."

"We're going abroad — for a year — perhaps longer. Vivien's fed up with this place. She never has cared for it, you know." He sighed; for a moment or two he looked downcast. Gerald Lee was very proud of his home. "Anyway, I've promised her a change. I've taken a villa near Algiers. A wonderful place, by all accounts." He laughed a little self-consciously. "Quite a second honeymoon, eh?"

For a minute or two Clare could not speak. Something seemed to be rising up in her throat and suffocating her. She could see the white walls of the villa, the orange trees, smell the soft perfumed breath of the South.

A second honeymoon!

They were going to escape. Vivien no longer believed in her threats. She was going away, carefree, gay, happy.

Clare heard her own voice, a little hoarse in timbre, saying the appropriate things. How lovely! She envied them!

Mercifully at that moment Rover and the spaniel decided to disagree. In the scuffle that ensued, further conversation was out of the question.

That afternoon Clare sat down and wrote a note to Vivien. She asked her to meet her on the Edge the following day, as she had something very important to say to her.

The next morning dawned bright and cloudless. Clare walked up the steep path of the Edge with a lightened heart. What a perfect day! She was glad that she had decided to say what had to be said out in the open, under the blue sky, instead of in her stuffy little sitting room. She was sorry for Vivien, very sorry indeed, but the thing had got to be done.

She saw a yellow dot, like some yellow flower higher up by the side of the path. As she came nearer, it resolved itself into the figure of Vivien, dressed in a yellow knitted frock, sitting on the short turf, her hands clasped round her knees.

"Good morning," said Clare. "Isn't it a perfect morning?"

"Is it?" said Vivien. "I haven't noticed. What was it you wanted to say to me?"

Clare dropped down on the grass beside her.

"I'm quite out of breath," she said apologetically. "It's a steep pull up here."

"Damn you!" cried Vivien shrilly. "Why can't you say it, you smooth-faced devil, instead of torturing me?"

Clare looked shocked, and Vivien hastily recanted.

"I didn't mean that. I'm sorry, Clare. I am indeed. Only — my nerves are all to pieces, and your sitting here and talking about the weather — well, it got me all rattled."

"You'll have a nervous breakdown if you're not careful," said Clare coldly.

Vivien gave a short laugh.

"Go over the edge? No — I'm not that kind. I'll never be a loony. Now tell me — what's all this about?"

Clare was silent for a moment, then she spoke, looking not at Vivien but steadily out over the sea.

"I thought it only fair to warn you that I can no longer keep silence about — about what happened last year."

28

"You mean — you'll go to Gerald with that story?"

"Unless you'll tell him yourself. That would be infinitely the better way."

Vivien laughed sharply.

"You know well enough I haven't got the pluck to do that."

Clare did not contradict the assertion. She had had proof before of Vivien's utterly craven temper.

"It would be infinitely better," she repeated.

Again Vivien gave that short, ugly laugh.

"It's your precious conscience, I suppose, that drives you to do this?" she sneered.

"I dare say it seems very strange to you," said Clare quietly. "But it honestly is that."

Vivien's white, set face stared into hers.

"My God!" she said. "I really believe you mean it, too. You actually think that's the reason."

"It *is* the reason."

"No, it isn't. If so, you'd have done it before — long ago. Why didn't you? No, don't answer. I'll tell you. You got more pleasure out of holding it over me — that's why. You liked to keep me on tenterhooks, and make me wince and squirm. You'd say things — diabolical things — just to torment me and keep me perpetually on the jump.

29

And so they did for a bit — till I got used to them."

"You got to feel secure," said Clare.

"You saw that, didn't you? But even then, you held back, enjoying your sense of power. But now we're going away, escaping from you, perhaps even going to be happy — you couldn't stick that at any price. So your convenient conscience wakes up!"

She stopped, panting. Clare said, still very quietly:

"I can't prevent your saying all these fantastical things, but I can assure you they're not true."

Vivien turned suddenly and caught her by the hand.

"Clare — for God's sake! I've been straight — I've done what you said. I've not seen Cyril again — I swear it."

"That's nothing to do with it."

"Clare — haven't you any pity — any kindness? I'll go down on my knees to you."

"Tell Gerald yourself. If you tell him, he may forgive you."

Vivien laughed scornfully.

"You know Gerald better than that. He'll be rabid — vindictive. He'll make me suffer — he'll make Cyril suffer. That's what I can't bear. Listen, Clare — he's doing so well.

He's invented something — machinery, I don't understand about it, but it may be a wonderful success. He's working it out now — his wife supplies the money for it, of course. But she's suspicious — jealous. If she finds out, and she will find out if Gerald starts proceedings for divorce — she'll chuck Cyril — his work, everything. Cyril will be ruined."

"I'm not thinking of Cyril," said Clare. "I'm thinking of Gerald. Why don't you think a little of him, too?"

"Gerald? I don't care that" — she snapped her fingers — "for Gerald. I never have. We might as well have the truth now we're at it. But I do care for Cyril. I'm a rotter, through and through, I admit it. I dare say he's a rotter, too. But my feeling for him — that *isn't* rotten. I'd die for him, do you hear? I'd die for him!"

"That is easily said," said Clare derisively.

"You think I'm not in earnest? Listen, if you go on with this beastly business, I'll kill myself. Sooner than have Cyril brought into it and ruined, I'd do that."

Clare remained unimpressed.

"You don't believe me?" said Vivien, panting.

"Suicide needs a lot of courage."

Vivien flinched back as though she had been struck.

"You've got me there. Yes, I've no pluck. If there were an easy way —"

"There's an easy way in front of you," said Clare. "You've only got to run straight down the green slope. It would be all over in a couple of minutes. Remember that child last year."

"Yes," said Vivien thoughtfully. "That would be easy — quite easy — if one really wanted to —"

Clare laughed.

Vivien turned to her.

"Let's have this out once more. Can't you see that by keeping silent as long as you have, you've — you've no right to go back on it now? I'll not see Cyril again. I'll be a good wife to Gerald — I swear I will. Or I'll go away and never see him again. Whichever you like. Clare —"

Clare got up.

"I advise you," she said, "to tell your husband yourself. . . . Otherwise — I shall."

"I see," said Vivien softly. "Well — I can't let Cyril suffer. . . ."

She got up — stood still as though considering for a minute or two, then ran lightly down to the path, but instead of stopping, crossed it and went down the slope. Once she half turned her head and waved a hand gaily to Clare, then she ran on gaily, lightly, as a child might run, out of sight. . . .

Clare stood petrified. Suddenly she heard cries, shouts, a clamor of voices. Then — silence.

She picked her way stiffly down to the path. About a hundred yards away a party of people coming up it had stopped. They were staring and pointing. Clare ran down and joined them.

"Yes, miss, someone's fallen over the cliff. Two men have gone down — to see."

She waited. Was it an hour, or eternity, or only a few minutes?

A man came toiling up the ascent. It was the vicar in his shirtsleeves. His coat had been taken off to cover what lay below.

"Horrible," he said, his face very white. "Mercifully, death must have been instantaneous."

He saw Clare, and came over to her.

"This must have been a terrible shock to you. You were taking a walk together, I understand?"

Clare heard herself answering mechanically.

Yes. They had just parted. No, Lady Lee's manner had been quite normal. One of the

33

group interposed the information that the lady was laughing and waving her hand. A terribly dangerous place — there ought to be a railing along the path.

The vicar's voice rose again.

"An accident — yes, clearly an accident."

And then suddenly Clare laughed — a hoarse, raucous laugh that echoed along the cliff.

"That's a damned lie," she said. *"I killed her."*

She felt someone patting her shoulder, a voice spoke soothingly.

"There, there. It's all right. You'll be all right presently."

But Clare was not all right presently. She was never all right again. She persisted in the delusion — certainly a delusion, since at least eight persons had witnessed the scene — that she had killed Vivien Lee.

She was very miserable till Nurse Lauriston came to take charge. Nurse Lauriston was very successful with mental cases.

"Humor them, poor things," she would say comfortably.

So she told Clare that she was a wardress from Pentonville Prison. Clare's sentence, she said, had been commuted to penal servitude for life. A room was fitted up as a cell.

34

"And now, I think, we shall be quite happy and comfortable," said Nurse Lauriston to the doctor. "Round-bladed knives if you like, doctor, but I don't think there's the least fear of suicide. She's not the type. Too self-centered. Funny how those are often the ones who go over the edge most easily."

II

The Actress

The shabby man in the fourth row of the pit leaned forward and stared incredulously at the stage. His shifty eyes narrowed furtively.

"Nancy Taylor!" he muttered. "By the Lord, little Nancy Taylor!"

His glance dropped to the program in his hand. One name was printed in slightly larger type than the rest.

"Olga Stormer! So that's what she calls herself. Fancy yourself a star, don't you, my lady? And you must be making a pretty little pot of money, too. Quite forgotten your name was ever Nancy Taylor, I daresay. I wonder now — I wonder now what you'd say if Jake Levitt should remind you of the fact?"

The curtain fell on the close of the first act. Hearty applause filled the auditorium. Olga Stormer, the great emotional actress, whose name in a few short years had become a household word, was adding yet another triumph to her list of successes as "Cora," in *The Avenging Angel*.

Jake Levitt did not join in the clapping, but a slow, appreciative grin gradually distended his mouth. God! What luck! Just when he was on his beam-ends, too. She'd try to bluff it out, he supposed, but she couldn't put it over on *him*. Properly worked, the thing was a gold mine!

On the following morning the first workings of Jake Levitt's gold mine became apparent. In her drawing room, with its red lacquer and black hangings, Olga Stormer read and reread a letter thoughtfully. Her pale face, with its exquisitely mobile features, was a little more set than usual, and every now and then the grey-green eyes under the level brows steadily envisaged the middle distance, as though she contemplated the threat behind rather than the actual words of the letter.

In that wonderful voice of hers, which could throb with emotion or be as clear cut as the click of a typewriter, Olga called: "Miss Jones!"

A neat young woman with spectacles, a shorthand pad and a pencil clasped in her hand, hastened from an adjoining room.

"Ring up Mr. Danahan, please, and ask him to come round, immediately."

Syd Danahan, Olga Stormer's manager,

entered the room with the usual apprehension of the man whose life it is to deal with and overcome the vagaries of the artistic feminine. To coax, to soothe, to bully, one at a time or all together, such was his daily routine. To his relief, Olga appeared calm and composed, and merely flicked a note across the table to him.

"Read that."

The letter was scrawled in an illiterate hand, on cheap paper.

> *Dear Madam,*
>
> *I much appreciated your performance in* The Avenging Angel *last night. I fancy we have a mutual friend in Miss Nancy Taylor, late of Chicago. An article regarding her is to be published shortly. If you would care to discuss same, I could call upon you at any time convenient to yourself.*
>
> *Yours respectfully,*
> *Jake Levitt*

Danahan looked slightly bewildered.

"I don't quite get it. Who is this Nancy Taylor?"

"A girl who would be better dead, Danny." There was bitterness in her voice and a weariness that revealed her thirty-four years. "A girl who was dead until this carrion crow brought her to life again."

"Oh! Then . . ."

"Me, Danny. Just me."

"This means blackmail, of course?"

She nodded. "Of course, and by a man who knows the art thoroughly."

Danahan frowned, considering the matter. Olga, her cheek pillowed on a long, slender hand, watched him with unfathomable eyes.

"What about bluff? Deny everything. He can't be sure that he hasn't been misled by a chance resemblance."

Olga shook her head.

"Levitt makes his living by blackmailing women. He's sure enough."

"The police?" hinted Danahan doubtfully.

Her faint, derisive smile was answer enough. Beneath her self-control, though he did not guess it, was the impatience of the keen brain watching a slower brain laboriously cover the ground it had already traversed in a flash.

"You don't — er — think it might be wise for you to — er — say something yourself to Sir Richard? That would partly spike his guns."

The actress's engagement to Sir Richard Everard, M.P., had been announced a few weeks previously.

"I told Richard everything when he asked me to marry him."

"My word, that was clever of you!" said Danahan admiringly.

Olga smiled a little.

"It wasn't cleverness, Danny dear. You wouldn't understand. All the same, if this man Levitt does what he threatens, my number is up, and incidentally Richard's Parliamentary career goes smash, too. No, as far as I can see, there are only two things to do."

"Well?"

"To pay — and that of course is endless! Or to disappear, start again."

The weariness was again very apparent in her voice.

"It isn't even as though I'd done anything I regretted. I was a half-starved little gutter waif, Danny, striving to keep straight. I shot a man, a beast of a man who deserved to be shot. The circumstances under which I killed him were such that no jury on earth would have convicted me. I know that now, but at the time I was only a frightened kid — and — I ran."

Danahan nodded.

"I suppose," he said doubtfully, "there's nothing against this man Levitt we could get hold of?"

Olga shook her head.

"Very unlikely. He's too much of a coward to go in for evildoing." The sound of her own words seemed to strike her. "A coward! I wonder if we couldn't work on that in some way."

"If Sir Richard were to see him and frighten him," suggested Danahan.

"Richard is too fine an instrument. You can't handle that sort of man with gloves on."

"Well, let me see him."

"Forgive me, Danny, but I don't think you're subtle enough. Something between gloves and bare fists is needed. Let us say mittens! That means a woman! Yes, I rather fancy a woman might do the trick. A woman with a certain amount of finesse, but who knows the baser side of life from bitter experience. Olga Stormer, for instance! Don't talk to me, I've got a plan coming."

She leaned forward, burying her face in her hands. She lifted it suddenly.

"What's the name of that girl who wants to understudy me? Margaret Ryan, isn't it? The girl with the hair like mine?"

"Her hair's all right," admitted Danahan grudgingly, his eyes resting on the bronze-gold coil surrounding Olga's head. "It's just like yours, as you say. But she's no good any other way. I was going to sack her next week."

"If all goes well, you'll probably have to let her understudy 'Cora.'" She smothered his protests with a wave of her hand. "Danny, answer me one question honestly. Do you think I can act? Really *act*, I mean. Or am I just an attractive woman who trails round in pretty dresses?"

"Act? My God! Olga, there's been nobody like you since Duse!"

"Then if Levitt is really a coward, as I suspect, the thing will come off. No, I'm not going to tell you about it. I want you to get hold of the Ryan girl. Tell her I'm interested in her and want her to dine here tomorrow night. She'll come fast enough."

"I should say she would!"

"The other thing I want is some good strong knockout drops, something that will put anyone out of action for an hour or two, but leave them none the worse the next day."

Danahan grinned.

"I can't guarantee our friend won't have a headache, but there will be no permanent damage done."

"Good! Run away now, Danny, and leave the rest to me." She raised her voice: "Miss Jones!"

The spectacled young woman appeared with her usual alacrity.

"Take down this, please."

Walking slowly up and down, Olga dictated the day's correspondence. But one answer she wrote with her own hand.

Jake Levitt, in his dingy room, grinned as he tore open the expected envelope.

Dear Sir,

I cannot recall the lady of whom you speak, but I meet so many people that my memory is necessarily uncertain. I am always pleased to help any fellow actress, and shall be at home if you will call this evening at nine o'clock.

 Yours faithfully,
 Olga Stormer

Levitt nodded appreciatively. Clever note! She admitted nothing. Nevertheless she was willing to treat. The gold mine was developing.

At nine o'clock precisely Levitt stood outside the door of the actress's flat and pressed the bell. No one answered the summons, and he was about to press it again when he realized that the door was not latched. He pushed the door open and entered the hall.

To his right was an open door leading into a brilliantly lighted room, a room decorated in scarlet and black. Levitt walked in. On the table under the lamp lay a sheet of paper on which were written the words: "Please wait until I return. — O. Stormer."

Levitt sat down and waited. In spite of himself a feeling of uneasiness was stealing over him. The flat was so very quiet. There was something eerie about the silence.

Nothing wrong, of course, how could there be? But the room was so deadly quiet; and yet, quiet as it was, he had the preposterous, uncomfortable notion that he wasn't alone in it. Absurd! He wiped the perspiration from his brow. And still the impression grew stronger. He wasn't alone! With a muttered oath he sprang up and began to pace up and down. In a minute the woman would return and then —

He stopped dead with a muffled cry. From beneath the black velvet hangings that draped the window a hand protruded! He stooped and touched it. Cold — horribly cold — a dead hand.

With a cry he flung back the curtains. A woman was lying there, one arm flung wide, the other doubled under her as she lay face downwards, her golden-bronze hair lying in dishevelled masses on her neck.

Olga Stormer! Tremblingly his fingers sought the icy coldness of that wrist and felt for the pulse. As he thought, there was none. She was dead. She had escaped him, then, by taking the simplest way out.

Suddenly his eyes were arrested by two ends of red cord finishing in fantastic tassels, and half hidden by the masses of her hair. He touched them gingerly; the head sagged as he did so, and he caught a glimpse of a horrible purple face. He sprang back with a cry, his head whirling. There was something here he did not understand. His brief glimpse of the face, disfigured as it was, had shown him one thing. This was murder, not suicide. The woman had been strangled and — she was not Olga Stormer!

Ah! What was that? A sound behind him. He wheeled round and looked straight into the terrified eyes of a maidservant crouching against the wall. Her face was as white as the cap and apron she wore, but he did not understand the fascinated horror in her eyes until her half-breathed words enlightened him to the peril in which he stood.

"Oh, my Gord! You've killed 'er!"

Even then he did not quite realize. He replied:

"No, no, she was dead when I found her."

"I saw yer do it! You pulled the cord and

strangled her. I 'eard the gurgling cry she give."

The sweat broke out upon his brow in earnest. His mind went rapidly over his actions of the previous few minutes. She must have come in just as he had the two ends of cord in his hands; she had seen the sagging head and had taken his own cry as coming from the victim. He stared at her helplessly. There was no doubting what he saw in her face — terror and stupidity. She would tell the police she had seen the crime committed, and no cross-examination would shake her, he was sure of that. She would swear away his life with the unshakable conviction that she was speaking the truth.

What a horrible, unforeseen chain of circumstances! Stop, was it unforeseen? Was there some devilry here? On an impulse he said, eyeing her narrowly: "That's not your mistress, you know."

Her answer, given mechanically, threw a light upon the situation.

"No, it's 'er actress friend — if you can call 'em friends, seeing that they fought like cat and dog. They were at it tonight, 'ammer and tongs."

A trap! He saw it now.

"Where's your mistress?"

"Went out ten minutes ago."

A trap! And he had walked into it like a lamb. A clever devil, this Olga Stormer; she had rid herself of a rival, and he was to suffer for the deed. Murder! My God, they hung a man for murder! And he was innocent — innocent!

A stealthy rustle recalled him. The little maid was sidling towards the door. Her wits were beginning to work again. Her eyes wavered to the telephone, then back to the door. At all costs he must silence her. It was the only way. As well hang for a real crime as a fictitious one. She had no weapon, neither had he. But he had his hands! Then his heart gave a leap. On the table beside her, almost under her hand, lay a small, jeweled revolver. If he could reach it first —

Instinct or his eyes warned her. She caught it up as he sprang and held it pointed at his breast. Awkwardly as she held it, her finger was on the trigger, and she could hardly miss him at that distance. He stopped dead. A revolver belonging to a woman like Olga Stormer would be pretty sure to be loaded.

But there was one thing, she was no longer directly behind him and the door. So long as he did not attack her, she might not have the nerve to shoot. Anyway, he must risk it. Zigzagging, he ran for the door, through the hall and out through the outer door, banging

47

it behind him. He heard her voice, faint and shaky, calling, 'Police, Murder!" She'd have to call louder than that before anyone was likely to hear her. He'd got a start, anyway. Down the stairs he went, running down the open street, then slacking to a walk as a stray pedestrian turned the corner. He had his plan cut and dried. To Gravesend as quickly as possible. A boat was sailing from there that night for the remoter parts of the world. He knew the captain, a man who, for a consideration, would ask no questions. Once on board and out to sea he would be safe.

At eleven o'clock Danahan's telephone rang. Olga's voice spoke.

"Prepare a contract for Miss Ryan, will you? She's to understudy 'Cora.' It's absolutely no use arguing. I owe her something after all the things I did to her tonight! What? Yes, I think I'm out of my troubles. By the way, if she tells you tomorrow that I'm an ardent spiritualist and put her into a trance tonight, don't show open incredulity. How? Knockout drops in the coffee, followed by scientific passes! After that I painted her face with purple grease paint and put a tourniquet on her left arm! Mystified? Well, you must stay mystified until tomorrow. I haven't time to explain now. I must get out of the cap and apron before my faithful Maud returns from the pictures. There was a 'beautiful drama' on tonight, she told me. But she missed the best drama of all. I played my best part tonight, Danny. The mittens won! Jake Levitt is a coward all right, and oh, Danny, Danny — I'm an actress!"

III

While the Light Lasts

The Ford car bumped from rut to rut, and the hot African sun poured down unmercifully. On either side of the so-called road stretched an unbroken line of trees and scrub, rising and falling in gently undulating lines as far as the eye could reach, the coloring a soft, deep yellow-green, the whole effect languorous and strangely quiet. Few birds stirred the slumbering silence. Once a snake wriggled across the road in front of the car, escaping the driver's efforts at destruction with sinuous ease. Once a native stepped out from the bush, dignified and upright, behind him a woman with an infant bound closely to her broad back and a complete household equipment, including a frying pan, balanced magnificently on her head.

All these things George Crozier had not failed to point out to his wife, who had answered him with a monosyllabic lack of attention which irritated him.

"Thinking of that fellow," he deduced

wrathfully. It was thus that he was wont to allude in his own mind to Deirdre Crozier's first husband, killed in the first year of the war. Killed, too, in the campaign against German West Africa. Natural she should, perhaps — he stole a glance at her, her fairness, the pink and white smoothness of her cheek, the rounded lines of her figure — rather more rounded perhaps than they had been in those far-off days when she had passively permitted him to become engaged to her, and then, in that first emotional scare of war, had abruptly cast him aside and made a war wedding of it with that lean, sunburned boy lover of hers, Tim Nugent.

Well, well, the fellow was dead — gallantly dead — and he, George Crozier, had married the girl he had always meant to marry. She was fond of him, too; how could she help it when he was ready to gratify her every wish and had the money to do it, too! He reflected with some complacency on his last gift to her, at Kimberley, where, owing to his friendship with some of the directors of De Beers, he had been able to purchase a diamond which, in the ordinary way, would not have been in the market, a stone not remarkable as to size, but of a very exquisite and rare shade, a peculiar deep amber, almost old gold, a diamond such as you might not find in a hundred years. And the look in her eyes when he gave it to her! Women were all the same about diamonds.

The necessity of holding on with both hands to prevent himself being jerked out brought George Crozier back to the realities. He ejaculated for perhaps the fourteenth time, with the pardonable irritation of a man who owns two Rolls-Royce cars and who has exercised his stud on the highways of civilization: "Good Lord, what a car! What a road!" He went on angrily: "Where the devil is this tobacco estate, anyway? It's over an hour since we left Bulawayo."

"Lost in Rhodesia," said Deirdre lightly between two involuntary leaps into the air.

But the coffee-colored driver, appealed to, responded with the cheering news that their destination was just round the next bend of the road.

The manager of the estate, Mr. Walters, was waiting on the stoop to receive them with the touch of deference due to George Crozier's prominence in Union Tobacco. He introduced his daughter-in-law, who shepherded Deirdre through the cool, dark inner hall to a bedroom beyond, where she could remove the veil with which she was always careful to shield her complexion when motoring. As she unfastened the pins in her usual leisurely, graceful fashion, Deirdre's eyes swept round the whitewashed ugliness of the bare room. No luxuries here, and Deirdre, who loved comfort as a cat loves cream, shivered a little. On the wall a text confronted her. "What shall it profit a man if he gain the whole world and lose his own soul?" it demanded of all and sundry, and Deirdre, pleasantly conscious that the question had nothing to do with her, turned to accompany her shy and rather silent guide. She noted, but not in the least maliciously, the spreading hips and the unbecoming cheap cotton gown. And with a glow of quiet appreciation her eyes dropped to the exquisite, costly simplicity of her own French white linen. Beautiful clothes, especially when worn by herself, roused in her the joy of the artist.

The two men were waiting for her.

"It won't bore you to come round, too, Mrs. Crozier?"

"Not at all. I've never been over a tobacco factory."

They stepped out into the still Rhodesian afternoon.

"These are the seedlings here; we plant them out as required. You see —"

The manager's voice droned on, interpolated by her husband's sharp staccato ques-

53

tions — output, stamp duty, problems of colored labor. She ceased to listen.

This was Rhodesia, this was the land Tim had loved, where he and she were to have gone together after the war was over. If he had not been killed! As always, the bitterness of revolt surged up in her at that thought. Two short months — that was all they had had. Two months of happiness — if that mingled rapture and pain were happiness. Was love ever happiness? Did not a thousand tortures beset the lover's heart? She had lived intensely in that short space, but had she ever known the peace, the leisure, the quiet contentment of her present life? And for the first time she admitted, somewhat unwillingly, that perhaps all had been for the best.

"I wouldn't have liked living out here. I mightn't have been able to make Tim happy. I might have disappointed him. George loves me, and I'm very fond of him, and he's very, very good to me. Why, look at that diamond he bought me only the other day." And, thinking of it, her eyelids drooped a little in pure pleasure.

"This is where we thread the leaves." Walters led the way into a low, long shed. On the floor were vast heaps of green leaves, and white-clad black "boys" squatted round them, picking and rejecting with deft fingers, sorting them into sizes, and stringing them by means of primitive needles on a long line of string. They worked with a cheerful leisureliness, jesting amongst themselves, and showing their white teeth as they laughed.

"Now, out here —"

They passed through the shed into the daylight again, where the lines of leaves hung drying in the sun. Deirdre sniffed delicately at the faint, almost imperceptible fragrance that filled the air.

Walters led the way into other sheds where the tobacco, kissed by the sun into faint yellow discoloration, underwent its further treatment. Dark here, with the brown swinging masses above, ready to fall to powder at a rough touch. The fragrance was stronger, almost overpowering it seemed to Deirdre, and suddenly a sort of terror came upon her, a fear of she knew not what, that drove her from that menacing, scented obscurity out into the sunlight. Crozier noted her pallor.

"What's the matter, my dear, don't you feel well? The sun, perhaps. Better not come with us round the plantations? Eh?"

Walters was solicitous. Mrs. Crozier had better go back to the house and rest. He called to a man a little distance away.

"Mr. Arden — Mrs. Crozier. Mrs. Crozier's feeling a little done up with the heat,

Arden. Just take her back to the house, will you?"

The momentary feeling of dizziness was passing. Deirdre walked by Arden's side. She had as yet hardly glanced at him.

"Deirdre!"

Her heart gave a leap, and then stood still. Only one person had ever spoken her name like that, with the faint stress on the first syllable that made of it a caress.

She turned and stared at the man by her side. He was burned almost black by the sun, he walked with a limp, and on the cheek nearer her was a long scar which altered his expression, but she knew him.

"Tim!"

For an eternity, it seemed to her, they gazed at each other, mute and trembling, and then, without knowing how or why, they were in each other's arms. Time rolled back for them. Then they drew apart again, and Deirdre, conscious as she put it of the idiocy of the question, said: "Then you're not dead?"

"No, they must have mistaken another chap for me. I was badly knocked on the head, but I came to and managed to crawl into the bush. After that I don't know what happened for months and months, but a friendly tribe looked after me, and at last I got my proper wits again and managed to get back to civilization." He paused. "I found you'd been married six months."

Deirdre cried out:

"Oh, Tim, understand, please understand! It was so awful, the loneliness — and the poverty. I didn't mind being poor with you, but when I was alone I hadn't the nerve to stand up against the sordidness of it all."

"It's all right, Deirdre; I did understand. I know you always have had a hankering after the fleshpots. I took you from them once — but the second time, well — my nerve failed. I was pretty badly broken up, you see, could hardly walk without a crutch, and then there was this scar."

She interrupted him passionately.

"Do you think I would have cared for that?"

"No, I know you wouldn't. I was a fool. Some women did mind, you know. I made up my mind I'd manage to get a glimpse of you. If you looked happy, if I thought you were contented to be with Crozier — why, then I'd remain dead. I did see you. You were just getting into a big car. You had on some lovely sable furs — things I'd never be able to give you if I worked my fingers to the bone — and — well — you seemed happy enough. I hadn't the same strength and courage, the same belief in myself, that I'd had before the war. All I could see was myself, broken and useless, barely able to earn enough to keep you — and you looked so beautiful, Deirdre, such a queen amongst women, so worthy to have furs and jewels and lovely clothes and all the hundred and one luxuries Crozier could give you. That — and — well, the pain — of seeing you together, decided me. Everyone believed me dead. I would stay dead."

"The pain!" repeated Deirdre in a low voice.

"Well, damn it all, Deirdre, it hurt! It isn't that I blame you. I don't. But it hurt."

They were both silent. Then Tim raised her face to his and kissed it with a new tenderness.

"But that's all over now, sweetheart. The only thing to decide is how we're going to break it to Crozier."

"Oh!" She drew herself away abruptly. "I hadn't thought —" She broke off as Crozier and the manager appeared round the angle of the path. With a swift turn of the head she whispered:

"Do nothing now. Leave it to me. I must prepare him. Where could I meet you tomorrow?"

Nugent reflected.

"I could come in to Bulawayo. How about the cafe near the Standard Bank? At three o'clock it would be pretty empty."

Deirdre gave a brief nod of assent before turning her back on him and joining the other two men. Tim Nugent looked after her with a faint frown. Something in her manner puzzled him.

Deirdre was very silent during the drive home. Sheltering behind the fiction of a "touch of the sun," she deliberated on her course of action. How should she tell him? How would he take it? A strange lassitude seemed to possess her, and a growing desire to postpone the revelation as long as might be. Tomorrow would be soon enough. There would be plenty of time before three o'clock.

The hotel was uncomfortable. Their room was on the ground floor, looking out onto an inner court. Deirdre stood that evening sniffing the stale air and glancing distastefully at the tawdry furniture. Her mind flew to the easy luxury of Monkton Court amidst the Surrey pinewoods. When her maid left her at last, she went slowly to her jewel case. In the palm of her hand the golden diamond returned her stare.

With an almost violent gesture she returned it to the case and slammed down the lid. Tomorrow morning she would tell George.

She slept badly. It was stifling beneath the heavy folds of the mosquito netting. The throbbing darkness was punctuated by the ubiquitous *ping* she had learned to dread. She awoke white and listless. Impossible to start a scene so early in the day!

She lay in the small, close room all the morning, resting. Lunchtime came upon her with a sense of shock. As they sat drinking coffee, George Crozier proposed a drive to the Matopos.

"Plenty of time if we start at once."

Deirdre shook her head, pleading a headache, and she thought to herself: "That settles it. I can't rush the thing. After all, what does a day more or less matter? I'll explain to Tim."

She waved good-bye to Crozier as he rattled off in the battered Ford. Then, glancing at her watch, she walked slowly to the meeting place.

The cafe was deserted at this hour. They sat down at a little table and ordered the inevitable tea that South Africa drinks at all hours of the day and night. Neither of them said a word till the waitress brought it and withdrew to her fastness behind some pink curtains. Then Deirdre looked up and started as she met the intense watchfulness in his eyes.

"Deirdre, have you told him?"

She shook her head, moistening her lips, seeking for words that would not come.

"Why not?"

"I haven't had a chance; there hasn't been time."

Even to herself the words sounded halting and unconvincing.

"It's not that. There's something else. I suspected it yesterday. I'm sure of it today. Deirdre, what is it?"

She shook her head dumbly.

"There's some reason why you don't want to leave George Crozier, why you don't want to come back to me. What is it?"

It was true. As he said it she knew it, knew it with sudden scorching shame, but knew it beyond any possibility of doubt. And still his eyes searched her.

"It isn't that you love him! You don't. But there's something."

She thought: "In another moment he'll see! Oh, God, don't let him!"

Suddenly his face whitened.

"Deirdre — is it — is it that there's going to be a — child?"

In a flash she saw the chance he offered

her. A wonderful way! Slowly, almost without her own volition, she bowed her head.

She heard his quick breathing, then his voice, rather high and hard.

"That — alters things. I didn't know. We've got to find a different way out." He leaned across the table and caught both her hands in his. "Deirdre, my darling, never think — never dream that you were in any way to blame. Whatever happens, remember that. I should have claimed you when I came back to England. I funked it, so it's up to me to do what I can to put things straight now. You see? Whatever happens, don't fret, darling. Nothing has been your fault."

He lifted first one hand, then the other to his lips. Then she was alone, staring at the untasted tea. And, strangely enough, it was only one thing that she saw — a gaudily illuminated text hanging on a whitewashed wall. The words seemed to spring out from it and hurl themselves at her. "What shall it profit a man —" She got up, paid for her tea, and went out.

On his return George Crozier was met by a request that his wife might not be disturbed. Her headache, the maid said, was very bad.

It was nine o'clock the next morning when he entered her bedroom, his face rather grave. Deirdre was sitting up in bed. She looked white and haggard, but her eyes shone.

"George, I've got something to tell you, something rather terrible —"

He interrupted her brusquely.

"So you've heard. I was afraid it might upset you."

"*Upset* me?"

"Yes. You talked to the poor young fellow that day."

He saw her hand steal to her heart, her eyelids flicker, then she said in a low, quick voice that somehow frightened him:

"I've heard nothing. Tell me quickly."

"I thought —"

"Tell me!"

"Out at that tobacco estate. Chap shot himself. Badly broken up in the war, nerves all to pieces, I suppose. There's no other reason to account for it."

"He shot himself — in that dark shed where the tobacco was hanging." She spoke with certainty, her eyes like a sleepwalker's as she saw before her in the odorous darkness a figure lying there, revolver in hand.

"Why, to be sure; that's where you were taken queer yesterday. Odd thing, that!"

Deirdre did not answer. She saw another picture — a table with tea things on it, and a woman bowing her head in acceptance of a lie.

"Well, well, the war has a lot to answer for," said Crozier, and stretched out his hand for a match, lighting his pipe with careful puffs.

His wife's cry startled him.

"Ah! don't, don't! I can't bear the smell!"

He stared at her in kindly astonishment.

"My dear girl, you mustn't be nervy. After all, you can't escape from the smell of tobacco. You'll meet it everywhere."

"Yes, everywhere!" She smiled a slow, twisted smile, and murmured some words that he did not catch, words that she had chosen for the original obituary notice of Tim Nugent's death. "While the light lasts I shall remember, and in the darkness I shall not forget."

Her eyes widened as they followed the ascending spiral of smoke, and she repeated in a low, monotonous voice: "Everywhere, everywhere."

IV

The House of Dreams

This is the story of John Segrave — of his life, which was unsatisfactory; of his love, which was unsatisfied; of his dreams, and of his death; and if in the two latter he found what was denied in the two former, then his life may, after all, be taken as a success. Who knows?

John Segrave came of a family which had been slowly going down the hill for the last century. They had been landowners since the days of Elizabeth, but their last piece of property was sold. It was thought well that one of the sons at least should acquire the useful art of money-making. It was an unconscious irony of Fate that John should be the one chosen.

With his strangely sensitive mouth, and the long dark blue slits of eyes that suggested an elf or a faun, something wild and of the woods, it was incongruous that he should be offered up, a sacrifice on the altar of Finance. The smell of the earth, the taste of the sea salt on one's lips, and the free sky above one's head — these were the things beloved by John Segrave, to which he was to bid farewell.

At the age of eighteen he became a junior clerk in a big business house. Seven years later he was still a clerk, not quite so junior, but with status otherwise unchanged. The faculty for "getting on in the world" had been omitted from his makeup. He was punctual, industrious, plodding — a clerk and nothing but a clerk.

And yet he might have been — what? He could hardly answer that question himself, but he could not rid himself of the conviction that somewhere there was a life in which he could have — counted. There was power in him, swiftness of vision, a something of which his fellow toilers had never had a glimpse. They liked him. He was popular because of his air of careless friendship, and they never appreciated the fact that he barred them out by that same manner from any real intimacy.

The dream came to him suddenly. It was no childish fantasy growing and developing through the years. It came on a midsummer night, or rather early morning, and he woke from it tingling all over, striving to hold it to him as it fled, slipping from his clutch in the elusive way dreams have.

Desperately he clung to it. It must not go

— it must not — He must remember the house. It was *the* House, of course! The House he knew so well. Was it a real house, or did he merely know it in dreams? He didn't remember — but he certainly knew it — knew it very well.

The faint grey light of the early morning was stealing into the room. The stillness was extraordinary. At 4:30 A.M. London, weary London, found her brief instant of peace.

John Segrave lay quiet, wrapped in the joy, the exquisite wonder and beauty of his dream. How clever it had been of him to remember it! A dream flitted so quickly as a rule, ran past you just as with waking consciousness your clumsy fingers sought to stop and hold it. But he had been too quick for this dream! He had seized it as it was slipping swiftly by him.

It was really a most remarkable dream! There was the house and — His thoughts were brought up with a jerk, for when he came to think of it, he couldn't remember anything but the house. And suddenly, with a tinge of disappointment, he recognized that, after all, the house was quite strange to him. He hadn't even dreamed of it before.

It was a white house, standing on high ground. There were trees near it, blue hills in the distance, but its peculiar charm was

67

independent of surroundings for (and this was the point, the climax of the dream) it was a beautiful, a strangely beautiful house. His pulses quickened as he remembered anew the strange beauty of the house.

The outside of it, of course, for he hadn't been inside. There had been no question of that — no question of it whatsoever.

Then, as the dingy outlines of his bed-sitting room began to take shape in the growing light, he experienced the disillusion of the dreamer. Perhaps, after all, his dream hadn't been so very wonderful — or had the wonderful, the explanatory part, slipped past him, and laughed at his ineffectual clutching hands? A white house, standing on high ground — there wasn't much there to get excited about, surely. It was rather a big house, he remembered, with a lot of windows in it, and the blinds were all down, not because the people were away (he was sure of that), but because it was so early that no one was up yet.

Then he laughed at the absurdity of his imaginings, and remembered that he was to dine with Mr. Wetterman that night.

Maisie Wetterman was Rudolf Wetterman's only daughter, and she had been accustomed all her life to having exactly what she wanted. Paying a visit to her father's office one day, she had noticed John Segrave. He had brought in some letters that her father had asked for. When he had departed again, she asked her father about him. Wetterman was communicative.

"One of Sir Edward Segrave's sons. Fine old family, but on its last legs. This boy will never set the Thames on fire. I like him all right, but there's nothing to him. No punch of any kind."

Maisie was, perhaps, indifferent to punch. It was a quality valued more by her parent than herself. Anyway, a fortnight later she persuaded her father to ask John Segrave to dinner. It was an intimate dinner, herself and her father, John Segrave, and a girlfriend who was staying with her.

The girlfriend was moved to make a few remarks.

"On approval, I suppose, Maisie? Later, father will do it up in a nice little parcel and bring it home from the city as a present to his dear little daughter, duly bought and paid for."

"Allegra! You are the limit."

Allegra Kerr laughed.

"You do take fancies, you know, Maisie. I like that hat — I must have it! If hats, why not husbands?"

"Don't be absurd. I've hardly spoken to him yet."

"No. But you've made up your mind," said the other girl. "What's the attraction, Maisie?"

"I don't know," said Maisie Wetterman slowly. "He's — different."

"Different?"

"Yes. I can't explain. He's good-looking, you know, in a queer sort of way, but it's not that. He's a way of not seeing you're there. Really, I don't believe he as much as glanced at me that day in father's office."

Allegra laughed.

"That's an old trick. Rather an astute young man, I should say."

"Allegra, you're hateful!"

"Cheer up, darling. Father will buy a woolly lamb for his little Maisiekins."

"I don't want it to be like that."

"Love with a capital L. Is that it?"

"Why shouldn't he fall in love with me?"

"No reason at all. I expect he will."

Allegra smiled as she spoke, and let her glance sweep over the other. Maisie Wetterman was short — inclined to be plump — she had dark hair, well shingled and artistically waved. Her naturally good complexion was enhanced by the latest colors in powder and lipstick. She had a good mouth and teeth, dark eyes, rather small and twinkly, and a jaw and chin slightly on the heavy side. She was beautifully dressed.

"Yes," said Allegra, finishing her scrutiny. "I've no doubt he will. The whole effect is really very good, Maisie."

Her friend looked at her doubtfully.

"I mean it," said Allegra. "I mean it — honor bright. But just supposing, for the sake of argument, that he shouldn't. Fall in love, I mean. Suppose his affection to become sincere, but platonic. What then?"

"I may not like him at all when I know him better."

"Quite so. On the other hand you may like him very much indeed. And in that latter case —"

Maisie shrugged her shoulders.

"I should hope I've too much pride —"

Allegra interrupted.

"Pride comes in handy for masking one's feelings — it doesn't stop you from feeling them."

"Well," said Maisie, flushed. "I don't see why I shouldn't say it. I *am* a very good match. I mean — from his point of view, father's daughter and everything."

"Partnership in the offing, et cetera," said Allegra. "Yes, Maisie. You're father's daughter, all right. I'm awfully pleased. I do like my friends to run true to type."

The faint mockery of her tone made the other uneasy.

"You are hateful, Allegra."

"But stimulating, darling. That's why you have me here. I'm a student of history, you know, and it always intrigued me why the court jester was permitted and encouraged. Now that I'm one myself, I see the point. It's rather a good role, you see, I had to do something. There was I, proud and penniless like the heroine of a novelette, well born and badly educated. 'What to do, girl? God wot,' saith she. The poor relation type of girl, all willingness to do without a fire in her room and content to do odd jobs and 'help dear Cousin So and So,' I observed to be at a premium. Nobody really wants her — except those people who can't keep their servants, and they treat her like a galley slave.

"So I became the court fool. Insolence, plain speaking, a dash of wit now and again (not too much lest I should have to live up to it), and behind it all, a very shrewd observation of human nature. People rather like being told how horrible they really are. That's why they flock to popular preachers. It's been a great success. I'm always overwhelmed with invitations. I can live on my friends with the greatest ease, and I'm careful to make no presence of gratitude."

"There's no one quite like you, Allegra. You don't mind in the least what you say."

"That's where you're wrong. I mind very much — I take care and thought about the matter. My seeming outspokenness is always calculated. I've got to be careful. This job has got to carry me on to old age."

"Why not marry? I know heaps of people have asked you."

Allegra's face grew suddenly hard.

"I can never marry."

"Because —" Maisie left the sentence unfinished, looking at her friend. The latter gave a short nod of assent.

Footsteps were heard on the stairs. The butler threw open the door and announced:

"Mr. Segrave."

John came in without any particular enthusiasm. He couldn't imagine why the old boy had asked him. If he could have got out of it he would have done so. The house depressed him, with its solid magnificence and the soft pile of its carpet.

A girl came forward and shook hands with him. He remembered vaguely having seen her one day in her father's office.

"How do you do, Mr. Segrave? Mr. Segrave — Miss Kerr."

Then he woke. Who was she? Where did

she come from? From the flame-colored draperies that floated round her, to the tiny Mercury wings on her small Greek head, she was a being transitory and fugitive, standing out against the dull background with an effect of unreality.

Rudolph Wetterman came in, his broad expanse of gleaming shirtfront creaking as he walked. They went down informally to dinner.

Allegra Kerr talked to her host. John Segrave had to devote himself to Maisie. But his whole mind was on the girl on the other side of him. She was marvelously effective. Her effectiveness was, he thought, more studied than natural. But behind all that, there lay something else. Flickering fire, fitful, capricious, like the will-o'-the-wisps that of old lured men into the marshes.

At last he got a chance to speak to her. Maisie was giving her father a message from some friend she had met that day. Now that the moment had come, he was tongue-tied. His glance pleaded with her dumbly.

"Dinner-table topics," she said lightly. "Shall we start with the theatres, or with one of those innumerable openings, beginning, 'Do you like — ?' "

John laughed.

"And if we find we both like dogs and

dislike sandy cats, it will form what is called a 'bond' between us?"

"Assuredly," said Allegra gravely.

"It is, I think, a pity to begin with a catechism."

"Yet it puts conversation within the reach of all."

"True, but with disastrous results."

"It is useful to know the rules — if only to break them."

John smiled at her.

"I take it, then, that you and I will indulge our personal vagaries. Even though we display thereby the genius that is akin to madness."

With a sharp unguarded movement, the girl's hand swept a wineglass off the table. There was the tinkle of broken glass. Maisie and her father stopped speaking.

"I'm so sorry, Mr. Wetterman. I'm throwing glasses on the floor."

"My dear Allegra, it doesn't matter at all, not at all."

Beneath his breath John Segrave said quickly:

"Broken glass. That's bad luck. I wish — it hadn't happened."

"Don't worry. How does it go? 'Ill luck thou canst not bring where ill luck has its home.' "

She turned once more to Wetterman. John, resuming conversation with Maisie, tried to place the quotation. He got it at last. They were the words used by Sieglinde in the *Walküre* when Sigmund offers to leave the house.

He thought: "Did she mean —"

But Maisie was asking his opinion of the latest revue. Soon he had admitted that he was fond of music.

"After dinner," said Maisie, "we'll make Allegra play for us."

They all went up to the drawing room together. Secretly, Wetterman considered it a barbarous custom. He liked the ponderous gravity of the wine passing round, the handed cigars. But perhaps it was as well tonight. He didn't know what on earth he could find to say to young Segrave. Maisie was too bad with her whims. It wasn't as though the fellow were good-looking — really good-looking — and certainly he wasn't amusing. He was glad when Maisie asked Allegra Kerr to play. They'd get through the evening sooner. The young idiot didn't even play bridge.

Allegra played well, though without the sure touch of a professional. She played modern music, Debussy and Strauss, a little Scriabine. Then she dropped into the first

76

movement of Beethoven's *Pathétique*, that expression of a grief that is infinite, a sorrow that is endless and vast as the ages, but in which from end to end breathes the spirit that will not accept defeat. In the solemnity of undying woe, it moves with the rhythm of the conqueror to its final doom.

Towards the end she faltered, her fingers struck a discord, and she broke off abruptly. She looked across at Maisie and laughed mockingly.

"You see," she said. "They won't let me."

Then, without waiting for a reply to her somewhat enigmatical remark, she plunged into a strange haunting melody, a thing of weird harmonies and curious measured rhythm, quite unlike anything Segrave had ever heard before. It was delicate as the flight of a bird, poised, hovering — Suddenly, without the least warning, it turned into a mere discordant jangle of notes, and Allegra rose laughing from the piano.

In spite of her laugh, she looked disturbed and almost frightened. She sat down by Maisie, and John heard the latter say in a low tone to her:

"You shouldn't do it. You really shouldn't do it."

"What was the last thing?" John asked eagerly.

"Something of my own."

She spoke sharply and curtly. Wetterman changed the subject.

That night John Segrave dreamed again of the House.

John was unhappy. His life was irksome to him as never before. Up to now he had accepted it patiently — a disagreeable necessity, but one which left his inner freedom essentially untouched. Now all that was changed. The outer world and the inner intermingled.

He did not disguise to himself the reason for the change. He had fallen in love at first sight with Allegra Kerr. What was he going to do about it?

He had been too bewildered that first night to make any plans. He had not even tried to see her again. A little later, when Maisie Wetterman asked him down to her father's place in the country for a weekend, he went eagerly, but he was disappointed, for Allegra was not there.

He mentioned her once, tentatively, to Maisie, and she told him that Allegra was up in Scotland paying a visit. He left it at that. He would have liked to go on talking about her, but the words seemed to stick in his throat.

Maisie was puzzled by him that weekend. He didn't appear to see — well, to see what was so plainly to be seen. She was a direct young woman in her methods, but directness was lost upon John. He thought her kind, but a little overpowering.

Yet the Fates were stronger than Maisie. They willed that John should see Allegra again.

They met in the park one Sunday afternoon. He had seen her from far off, and his heart thumped against the side of his ribs. Supposing she should have forgotten him —

But she had not forgotten. She stopped and spoke. In a few minutes they were walking side by side, striking out across the grass. He was ridiculously happy.

He said suddenly and unexpectedly: "Do you believe in dreams?"

"I believe in nightmares."

The harshness of her voice startled him.

"Nightmares," he said stupidly. "I didn't mean nightmares."

Allegra looked at him.

"No," she said. "There have been no nightmares in your life. I can see that."

Her voice was gentle — different —

He told her then of his dream of the white house, stammering a little. He had had it now six — no, seven times. Always the same.

It was beautiful — so beautiful!

He went on.

"You see — it's to do with *you* — in some way. I had it first the night before I met you —"

"To do with me?" She laughed — a short bitter laugh. "Oh, no, that's impossible. The house was beautiful."

"So are you," said John Segrave.

Allegra flushed a little with annoyance.

"I'm sorry — I was stupid. I seemed to ask for a compliment, didn't I? But I didn't really mean that at all. The outside of me is all right, I know."

"I haven't seen the inside of the house yet," said John Segrave. "When I do I know it will be quite as beautiful as the outside."

He spoke slowly and gravely, giving the words a meaning that she chose to ignore.

"There is something more I want to tell you — if you will listen."

"I will listen," said Allegra.

"I am chucking up this job of mine. I ought to have done it long ago — I see that now. I have been content to drift along knowing I was an utter failure, without caring much, just living from day to day. A man shouldn't do that. It's a man's business to find something he can do and make a success of it. I'm chucking this, and taking on some-

80

thing else — quite a different sort of thing. it's a kind of expedition in West Africa — I can't tell you the details. They're not supposed to be known; but if it comes off — well, I shall be a rich man."

"So you, too, count success in terms of money?"

"Money," said John Segrave, "means just one thing to me — you! When I come back —" he paused.

She bent her head. Her face had grown very pale.

"I won't pretend to misunderstand. That's why I must tell you now, once and for all: *I shall never marry.*"

He stayed a little while considering, then he said very gently:

"Can't you tell me why?"

"I could, but more than anything in the world I want not to tell you."

Again he was silent, then he looked up suddenly and a singularly attractive smile illumined his faun's face.

"I see," he said. "So you won't let me come inside the House — not even to peep in for a second? The blinds are to stay down."

Allegra leaned forward and laid her hand on his.

"I will tell you this much. You dream of

your House. But I — I don't dream. My dreams are nightmares!"

And on that she left him, abruptly, disconcertingly.

That night, once more, he dreamed. Of late, he had realized that the House was most certainly tenanted. He had seen a hand draw aside the blinds, had caught glimpses of moving figures within.

Tonight the House seemed fairer than it had ever done before. Its white walls shone in the sunlight. The peace and the beauty of it were complete.

Then, suddenly, he became aware of a fuller ripple of the waves of joy. Someone was coming to the window. He knew it. A hand, the same hand that he had seen before, laid hold of the blind, drawing it back. In a minute he would see —

He was awake — still quivering with the horror, the unutterable loathing of the *Thing* that had looked out at him from the window of the House.

It was a Thing utterly and wholly horrible, a Thing so vile and loathsome that the mere remembrance of it made him feel sick. And he knew that the most unutterably and horribly vile thing about it was its presence in that House — the House of Beauty.

For where that Thing abode was horror — horror that rose up and slew the peace and the serenity which were the birthright of the House. The beauty, the wonderful immortal beauty of the House was destroyed for ever, for within its holy consecrated walls there dwelt the Shadow of an Unclean Thing!

If ever again he should dream of the House, Segrave knew he would awake at once with a start of terror, lest from its white beauty that Thing might suddenly look out at him.

The following evening, when he left the office, he went straight to the Wettermans' house. He must see Allegra Kerr. Maisie would tell him where she was to be found.

He never noticed the eager light that flashed into Maisie's eyes as he was shown in, and she jumped up to greet him. He stammered out his request at once, with her hand still in his.

"Miss Kerr. I met her yesterday, but I don't know where she's staying."

He did not feel Maisie's hand grow limp in his as she withdrew it. The sudden coldness of her voice told him nothing.

"Allegra is here — staying with us. But I'm afraid you can't see her."

"But —"

"You see, her mother died this morning.

83

We've just had the news."

"Oh!" He was taken aback.

"It is all very sad," said Maisie. She hesitated just a minute, then went on. "You see, she died in — well, practically an asylum. There's insanity in the family. The grandfather shot himself, and one of Allegra's aunts is a hopeless imbecile, and another drowned herself."

John Segrave made an inarticulate sound.

"I thought I ought to tell you," said Maisie virtuously. "We're such friends, aren't we? And of course Allegra is very attractive. Lots of people have asked her to marry them, but naturally she won't marry at all — she couldn't, could she?"

"She's all right," said Segrave. "There's nothing wrong with *her*."

His voice sounded hoarse and unnatural in his own ears.

"One never knows; her mother was quite all right when she was young. And she wasn't just — peculiar, you know. She was quite raving mad. It's a dreadful thing — insanity."

"Yes," he said, "it's a most awful Thing —"

He knew now what it was that had looked at him from the window of the House.

Maisie was still talking on. He interrupted her brusquely.

"I really came to say good-bye — and to thank you for all your kindness."

"You're not — going away?"

There was alarm in her voice.

He smiled sideways at her — a crooked smile, pathetic and attractive.

"Yes," he said. "To Africa."

"Africa!"

Maisie echoed the word blankly. Before she could pull herself together he had shaken her by the hand and gone. She was left standing there, her hands clenched by her sides, an angry spot of color in each cheek.

Below, on the doorstep, John Segrave came face to face with Allegra coming in from the street. She was in black, her face white and lifeless. She took one glance at him then drew him into a small morning room.

"Maisie told you," she said. "You *know?*"

He nodded.

"But what does it matter? *You're* all right. It — it leaves some people out."

She looked at him somberly, mournfully.

"You *are* all right," he repeated.

"I don't know," she almost whispered it. "I don't know. I told you — about my dreams. And when I play — when I'm at the piano — *those others* come and take hold of my hands."

85

He was staring at her — paralyzed. For one instant, as she spoke, something looked out from her eyes. It was gone in a flash — but he knew it. It was the Thing that had looked out from the House.

She caught his momentary recoil.

"You see," she whispered. "You see — But I wish Maisie hadn't told you. It takes everything from you."

"Everything?"

"Yes. There won't even be the dreams left. For now — you'll never dare to dream of the House again."

The West African sun poured down, and the heat was intense.

John Segrave continued to moan.

"I can't find it. I can't find it."

The little English doctor with the red head and the tremendous jaw scowled down upon his patient in that bullying manner which he had made his own.

"He's always saying that. What does he mean?"

"He speaks, I think, of a house, monsieur." The soft-voiced Sister of Charity from the Roman Catholic Mission spoke with her gentle detachment, as she too looked down on the stricken man.

"A house, eh? Well, he's got to get it out

86

of his head, or we shan't pull him through. It's on his mind. Segrave! Segrave!"

The wandering attention was fixed. The eyes rested with recognition on the doctor's face.

"Look here, you're going to pull through. I'm going to pull you through. But you've got to stop worrying about this house. It can't run away, you know. So don't bother about looking for it now."

"All right." He seemed obedient. "I suppose it can't very well run away if it's never been there at all."

"Of course not!" The doctor laughed his cheery laugh. "Now you'll be all right in no time." And with a boisterous bluntness of manner he took his departure.

Segrave lay thinking. The fever had abated for the moment, and he could think clearly and lucidly. He *must* find that House.

For ten years he had dreaded finding it — the thought that he might come upon it unawares had been his greatest terror. And then, he remembered, when his fears were quite lulled to rest, one day *it* had found *him*. He recalled clearly his first haunting terror, and then his sudden, his exquisite, relief. For, after all, the House was empty!

Quite empty and exquisitely peaceful. It was as he remembered it ten years before.

He had not forgotten. There was a huge black furniture van moving slowly away from the House. The last tenant, of course, moving out with his goods. He went up to the men in charge of the van and spoke to them. There was something rather sinister about that van, it was so very black. The horses were black, too, with freely flowing manes and tails, and the men all wore black clothes and gloves. It all reminded him of something else, something that he couldn't remember.

Yes, he had been quite right. The last tenant was moving out, as his lease was up. The House was to stand empty for the present, until the owner came back from abroad.

And waking, he had been full of the peaceful beauty of the empty House.

A month after that, he had received a letter from Maisie (she wrote to him perseveringly, once a month). In it she told him that Allegra Kerr had died in the same home as her mother, and wasn't it dreadfully sad? Though of course a merciful release.

It had really been very odd indeed. Coming after his dream like that. He didn't quite understand it all. But it was odd.

And the worst of it was that he'd never been able to find the House since. Somehow, he'd forgotten the way.

The fever began to take hold of him once

more. He tossed restlessly. Of course, he'd forgotten, the House was on high ground! He must climb to get there. But it was hot work climbing cliffs — dreadfully hot. Up, up, up — Oh! he had slipped! He must start again from the bottom. Up, up, up — days passed, weeks — he wasn't sure that years didn't go by! And he was still climbing.

Once he heard the doctor's voice. But he couldn't stop climbing to listen. Besides the doctor would tell him to leave off looking for the House. *He* thought it was an ordinary house. He didn't know.

He remembered suddenly that he must be calm, very calm. You couldn't find the House unless you were very calm. It was no use looking for the House in a hurry, or being excited.

If he could only keep calm! But it was so hot! Hot? It was *cold* — yes, cold. These weren't cliffs, they were icebergs — jagged, cold icebergs.

He was so tired. He wouldn't go on looking — it was no good — Ah! here was a lane — that was better than icebergs, anyway. How pleasant and shady it was in the cool, green lane. And those trees — they were splendid! They were rather like — what? He couldn't remember, but it didn't matter.

Ah! here were flowers. All golden and

blue! How lovely it all was — and how strangely familiar. Of course, he had been here before. There, through the trees, was the gleam of the House, standing on the high ground. How beautiful it was. The green lane and the trees and the flowers were as nothing to the paramount, the all-satisfying beauty of the House.

He hastened his steps. To think that he had never yet been inside! How unbelievably stupid of him — when he had the key in his pocket all the time!

And of course the beauty of the exterior was as nothing to the beauty that lay within — especially now that the Owner had come back from abroad. He mounted the steps to the great door.

Cruel strong hands were dragging him back! They fought him, dragging him to and fro, backwards and forwards.

The doctor was shaking him, roaring in his ear. "Hold on, man, you can. Don't let go. Don't let go." His eyes were alight with the fierceness of one who sees an enemy. Segrave wondered who the Enemy was. The black-robed nun was praying. That, too, was strange.

And all *he* wanted was to be left alone. To go back to the House. For every minute the House was growing fainter.

That, of course, was because the doctor was so strong. He wasn't strong enough to fight the doctor. If he only could.

But stop! There was another way — the way dreams went in the moment of waking. No strength could stop *them* — they just flitted past. The doctor's hands wouldn't be able to hold him if he slipped — just slipped!

Yes, that was the way! The white walls were visible once more, the doctor's voice was fainter, his hands were barely felt. He knew now how dreams laugh when they give you the slip!

He was at the door of the House. The exquisite stillness was unbroken. He put the key in the lock and turned it.

Just a moment he waited, to realize to the full the perfect, the ineffable, the all-satisfying completeness of joy.

Then — he passed over the Threshold.

V

The Lonely God

He stood on a shelf in the British Museum, alone and forlorn amongst a company of obviously more important deities. Ranged round the four walls, these greater personages all seemed to display an overwhelming sense of their own superiority. The pedestal of each was duly inscribed with the land and race that had been proud to possess him. There was no doubt of their position; they were divinities of importance and recognized as such.

Only the little god in the corner was aloof and remote from their company. Roughly hewn out of grey stone, his features almost totally obliterated by time and exposure, he sat there in isolation, his elbows on his knees, and his head buried in his hands; a lonely little god in a strange country.

There was no inscription to tell the land whence he came. He was indeed lost, without honor or renown, a pathetic little figure very far from home. No one noticed him, no one stopped to look at him. Why should they? He was so insignificant, a block of grey stone in a corner. On either side of him were two Mexican gods worn smooth with age, placid idols with folded hands, and cruel mouths curved in a smile that showed openly their contempt of humanity. There was also a rotund, violently self-assertive little god, with a clenched fist, who evidently suffered from a swollen sense of his own importance, but passersby stopped to give him a glance sometimes, even if it was only to laugh at the contrast of his absurd pomposity with the smiling indifference of his Mexican companions.

And the little lost god sat on there hopelessly, his head in his hands, as he had sat year in and year out, till one day the impossible happened, and he found — a worshipper.

"Any letters for me?"

The hall porter removed a packet of letters from a pigeonhole, gave a cursory glance through them, and said in a wooden voice:

"Nothing for you, sir."

Frank Oliver sighed as he walked out of the club again. There was no particular reason why there should have been anything for him. Very few people wrote to him. Ever since he had returned from Burma in the spring, he had become conscious of a growing and increasing loneliness.

Frank Oliver was a man just over forty, and the last eighteen years of his life had been spent in various parts of the globe, with brief furloughs in England. Now that he had retired and come home to live for good, he realized for the first time how very much alone in the world he was.

True, there was his sister Greta, married to a Yorkshire clergyman, very busy with parochial duties and the bringing up of a family of small children. Greta was naturally very fond of her only brother, but equally naturally she had very little time to give him. Then there was his old friend Tom Hurley. Tom was married to a nice, bright, cheerful girl, very energetic and practical, of whom Frank was secretly afraid. She told him brightly that he must not be a crabbed old bachelor, and was always producing "nice girls." Frank Oliver found that he never had anything to say to these "nice girls"; they persevered with him for a while, then gave him up as hopeless.

And yet he was not really unsociable. He had a great longing for companionship and sympathy, and ever since he had been back in England he had become aware of a growing discouragement. He had been away too long, he was out of tune with the times. He spent long, aimless days wandering about, wondering what on earth he was to do with himself next.

It was on one of these days that he strolled into the British Museum. He was interested in Asiatic curiosities, and so it was that he chanced upon the lonely god. Its charm held him at once. Here was something vaguely akin to himself; here, too, was someone lost and astray in a strange land. He became in the habit of paying frequent visits to the Museum, just to glance in on the little grey stone figure, in its obscure place on the high shelf.

"Rough luck on the little chap," he thought to himself. "Probably had a lot of fuss made about him once, kowtowing and offerings and all the rest of it."

He had begun to feel such a proprietary right in his little friend (it really almost amounted to a sense of actual ownership) that he was inclined to be resentful when he found that the little god had made a second conquest. *He* had discovered the lonely god; nobody else, he felt, had a right to interfere.

But after the first flash of indignation, he was forced to smile at himself. For this second worshipper was such a little bit of a thing, such a ridiculous, pathetic creature, in a shabby black coat and skirt that had seen their best days. She was young, a little over twenty he should judge, with fair hair and blue eyes, and a wistful droop to her mouth.

Her hat especially appealed to his chivalry. She had evidently trimmed it herself, and it made such a brave attempt to be smart that its failure was pathetic. She was obviously a lady, though a poverty-stricken one, and he immediately decided in his own mind that she was a governess and alone in the world.

He soon found out that her days for visiting the god were Tuesdays and Fridays, and she always arrived at ten o'clock, as soon as the Museum was open. At first he disliked her intrusion, but little by little it began to form one of the principal interests of his monotonous life. Indeed, the fellow devotee was fast ousting the object of devotion from his position of preeminence. The days that he did not see the "Little Lonely Lady," as he called her to himself, were blank.

Perhaps she, too, was equally interested in him, though she endeavored to conceal the fact with studious unconcern. But little by little a sense of fellowship was slowly growing between them, though as yet they had exchanged no spoken word. The truth of the matter was, the man was too shy! He argued to himself that very likely she had not even noticed him (some inner sense gave the lie to that instantly), that she would consider it a great impertinence, and, finally, that he had not the least idea what to say.

But Fate, or the little god, was kind, and sent him an inspiration — or what he regarded as such. With infinite delight in his own cunning, he purchased a woman's handkerchief, a frail little affair of cambric and lace which he almost feared to touch, and, thus armed, he followed her as she departed, and stopped her in the Egyptian room.

"Excuse me, but is this yours?" He tried to speak with airy unconcern, and signally failed.

The Lonely Lady took it, and made a pretence of examining it with minute care.

"No, it is not mine." She handed it back, and added, with what he felt guiltily was a suspicious glance: "It's quite a new one. The price is still on it."

But he was unwilling to admit that he had been found out. He started on an over-plausible flow of explanation.

"You see, I picked it up under that big case. It was just by the farthest leg of it." He derived great relief from this detailed account. "So, as you had been standing there, I thought it must be yours and came after you with it."

She said again: "No, it isn't mine," and

added, as if with a sense of ungraciousness, "Thank you."

The conversation came to an awkward standstill. The girl stood there, pink and embarrassed, evidently uncertain how to retreat with dignity.

He made a desperate effort to take advantage of his opportunity.

"I — I didn't know there was anyone else in London who cared for our little lonely god till you came."

She answered eagerly, forgetting her reserve: "Do *you* call him that too?"

Apparently, if she had noticed his pronoun, she did not resent it. She had been startled into sympathy, and his quiet "Of course!" seemed the most natural rejoinder in the world.

Again there was a silence, but this time it was a silence born of understanding.

It was the lonely Lady who broke it in a sudden remembrance of the conventionalities.

She drew herself up to her full height, and with an almost ridiculous assumption of dignity for so small a person, she observed in chilling accents: "I must be going now. Good morning." And with a slight, stiff inclination of her head, she walked away, holding herself very erect.

★ ★ ★

By all acknowledged standards Frank Oliver ought to have felt rebuffed, but it is a regrettable sign of his rapid advance in depravity that he merely murmured to himself: "Little darling!"

He was soon to repent of his temerity, however. For ten days his little lady never came near the Museum. He was in despair! He had frightened her away! She would never come back! He was a brute, a villain! He would never see her again!

In his distress he haunted the British Museum all day long. She might merely have changed her time of coming. He soon began to know the adjacent rooms by heart, and he contracted a lasting hatred of mummies. The guardian policeman observed him with suspicion when he spent three hours poring over Assyrian hieroglyphics, and the contemplation of endless vases of all ages nearly drove him mad with boredom.

But one day his patience was rewarded. She came again, rather pinker than usual, and trying hard to appear self-possessed.

He greeted her with cheerful friendliness.

"Good morning. It is ages since you've been here."

"Good morning."

She let the words slip out with icy frigidity,

99

and coldly ignored the end part of his sentence.

But he was desperate.

"Look here!" He stood confronting her with pleading eyes that reminded her irresistibly of a large, faithful dog. "Won't you be friends? I'm all alone in London — all alone in the world, and I believe you are, too. We ought to be friends. Besides, our little god has introduced us."

She looked up half doubtfully, but there was a faint smile quivering at the corners of her mouth.

"Has he?"

"Of course!"

It was the second time he had used this extremely positive form of assurance, and now, as before, it did not fail of its effect, for after a minute or two the girl said, in that slightly royal manner of hers:

"Very well."

"That's splendid," he replied gruffly, but there was something in his voice as he said it that made the girl glance at him swiftly, with a sharp impulse of pity.

And so the queer friendship began. Twice a week they met, at the shrine of a little heathen idol. At first they confined their conversation solely to him. He was, as it were, at once a palliation of, and an excuse for, their friendship. The question of his origin was widely discussed. The man insisted on attributing to him the most bloodthirsty characteristics. He depicted him as the terror and dread of his native land, insatiable for human sacrifice, and bowed down to by his people in fear and trembling. In the contrast between his former greatness and his present insignificance there lay, according to the man, all the pathos of the situation.

The Lonely Lady would have none of this theory. He was essentially a kind little god, she insisted. She doubted whether he had ever been very powerful. If he had been so, she argued, he would not now be lost and friendless, and, anyway, he was a dear little god, and she loved him, and she hated to think of him sitting there day after day with all those other horrid, supercilious things jeering at him, because you could see they did! After this vehement outburst the little lady was quite out of breath.

That topic exhausted, they naturally began to talk of themselves. He found out that his surmise was correct. She was a nursery governess to a family of children who lived at Hampstead. He conceived an instant dislike of these children; of Ted, who was five and really not *naughty*, only mischievous; of the twins who *were* rather trying, and of Molly, who wouldn't do anything she was told, but was such a dear you couldn't be cross with her!

"Those children bully you," he said grimly and accusingly to her.

"They do not," she retorted with spirit. "I am extremely stern with them."

"Oh! Ye gods!" he laughed. But she made him apologize humbly for his skepticism.

She was an orphan, she told him, quite alone in the world.

Gradually he told her something of his own life: of his official life, which had been painstaking and mildly successful; and of his unofficial pastime, which was the spoiling of yards of canvas.

"Of course, I don't know anything about it," he explained. "But I have always felt I could paint something someday. I can sketch pretty decently, but I'd like to do a real picture of something. A chap who knew once told me that my technique wasn't bad."

She was interested, pressed for details.

"I am sure you paint awfully well."

He shook his head.

"No, I've begun several things lately and chucked them up in despair. I always thought that, when I had the time, it would be plain sailing. I have been storing up that idea for years, but now, like everything else,

I suppose, I've left it too late."

"Nothing's too late — ever," said the little lady, with the vehement earnestness of the very young.

He smiled down on her. "You think not, child? It's too late for some things for me."

And the little lady laughed at him and nicknamed him Methuselah.

They were beginning to feel curiously at home in the British Museum. The solid and sympathetic policeman who patrolled the galleries was a man of tact, and on the appearance of the couple he usually found that his onerous duties of guardianship were urgently needed in the adjoining Assyrian room.

One day the man took a bold step. He invited her out to tea!

At first she demurred.

"I have no time. I am not free. I can come some mornings because the children have French lessons."

"Nonsense," said the man. "You could manage one day. Kill off an aunt or a second cousin or something, but *come*. We'll go to a little ABC shop near here, and have buns for tea! I know you must love buns!"

"Yes, the penny kind with currants!"

"And a lovely glaze on top —"

"They are such plump, dear things —"

"There is something," Frank Oliver said solemnly, "infinitely comforting about a bun!"

So it was arranged, and the little governess came, wearing quite an expensive hothouse rose in her belt in honor of the occasion.

He had noticed that, of late, she had a strained, worried look, and it was more apparent than ever this afternoon as she poured out the tea at the little marble-topped table.

"Children been bothering you?" he asked solicitously.

She shook her head. She had seemed curiously disinclined to talk about the children lately.

"*They're* all right. I never mind them."

"Don't you?"

His sympathetic tone seemed to distress her unwarrantably.

"Oh, no. It was never that. But — but, indeed, I was lonely. I was indeed!" Her tone was almost pleading.

He said quickly, touched: "Yes, yes, child. I know — I know."

After a minute's pause he remarked in a cheerful tone: "Do you know, you haven't even asked my name yet?"

She held up a protesting hand.

"Please, I don't want to know it. And don't ask mine. Let us be just two lonely people who've come together and made friends. It makes it so much more wonderful — and — and different."

He said slowly and thoughtfully: "Very well. In an otherwise lonely world we'll be two people who have just each other."

It was a little different from her way of putting it, and she seemed to find it difficult to go on with the conversation. Instead, she bent lower and lower over her plate, till only the crown of her hat was visible.

"That's rather a nice hat," he said by way of restoring her equanimity.

"I trimmed it myself," she informed him proudly.

"I thought so the moment I saw it," he answered, saying the wrong thing with cheerful ignorance.

"I'm afraid it is not as fashionable as I meant it to be!"

"I think it's a perfectly lovely hat," he said loyally.

Again constraint settled down upon them. Frank Oliver broke the silence bravely.

"Little Lady, I didn't mean to tell you yet, but I can't help it. I love you. I want you. I loved you from the first moment I saw you standing there in your little black suit. Dearest, if two lonely people were together — why — there would be no more loneliness.

And I'd work, oh! how I'd work! I'd paint you. I could, I know I could. Oh! my little girl, I can't live without you. I can't indeed —"

His little lady was looking at him very steadily. But what she said was quite the last thing he expected her to say. Very quietly and distinctly she said: "You *bought* that handkerchief!"

He was amazed at this proof of feminine perspicacity, and still more amazed at her remembering it against him now. Surely, after this lapse of time, it might have been forgiven him.

"Yes, I did," he acknowledged humbly. "I wanted an excuse to speak to you. Are you very angry?" He waited meekly for her words of condemnation.

"I think it was sweet of you!" cried the little lady with vehemence. "Just sweet of you!" her voice ended uncertainly.

Frank Oliver went on in his gruff tone:

"Tell me, child, is it impossible? I know I'm an ugly, rough old fellow —"

The Lonely Lady interrupted him.

"No, you're not! I wouldn't have you different, not in any way. I love you just as you are, do you understand? Not because I'm sorry for you, not because I'm alone in the world and want someone to be fond of me and take care of me — but because you're just — *you.* Now do you understand?"

"Is it true?" he asked half in a whisper.

And she answered steadily: "Yes, it's true —" The wonder of it overpowered them.

At last he said whimsically: "So we've fallen upon heaven, dearest!"

"In an ABC shop," she answered in a voice that held tears and laughter.

But terrestrial heavens are short-lived. The little lady started up with an exclamation.

"I'd no idea how late it was! I must go at once."

"I'll see you home."

"No, no, *no!*"

He was forced to yield to her insistence, and merely accompanied her as far as the Tube station.

"Good-bye, dearest." She clung to his hand with an intensity that he remembered afterwards.

"Only good-bye till tomorrow," he answered cheerfully. "Ten o'clock as usual, and we'll tell each other our names and our histories, and be frightfully practical and prosaic."

"Good-bye to — heaven, though," she whispered.

"It will be with us always, sweetheart!"

She smiled back at him, but with that same sad appeal that disquieted him and which he could not fathom. Then the relentless lift dragged her down out of sight.

He was strangely disturbed by those last words of hers, but he put them resolutely out of his mind and substituted radiant anticipations of tomorrow in their stead.

At ten o'clock he was there, in the accustomed place. For the first time he noticed how malevolently the other idols looked down upon him. It almost seemed as if they were possessed of some secret evil knowledge affecting him, over which they were gloating. He was uneasily aware of their dislike.

The little lady was late. Why didn't she come? The atmosphere of this place was getting on his nerves. Never had his own little friend (*their* god) seemed so hopelessly impotent as today. A helpless lump of stone, hugging his own despair!

His cogitations were interrupted by a small, sharp-faced boy who had stepped up to him, and was earnestly scrutinizing him from head to foot. Apparently satisfied with the result of his observations, he held out a letter.

"For me?"

It had no superscription. He took it, and the sharp boy decamped with extraordinary rapidity.

Frank Oliver read the letter slowly and unbelievingly. It was quite short.

Dearest,
I can never marry you. Please forget that I ever came into your life at all, and try to forgive me if I have hurt you. Don't try to find me, because it will be no good. It is really "good-bye."
The Lonely Lady

There was a postscript which had evidently been scribbled at the last moment:

I do love you. I do indeed.

And that little impulsive postscript was all the comfort he had in the weeks that followed. Needless to say, he disobeyed her injunction "not to try to find her," but all in vain. She had vanished completely, and he had no clue to trace her by. He advertised despairingly, imploring her in veiled terms at least to explain the mystery, but blank silence rewarded his efforts. She was gone, never to return.

And then it was that for the first time in his life he really began to paint. His technique had always been good. Now craftsmanship and inspiration went hand in hand.

The picture that made his name and brought him renown was accepted and hung in the Academy, and was accounted to be *the* picture of the year, no less for the exquisite treatment of the subject than for the masterly workmanship and technique. A certain amount of mystery, too, rendered it more interesting to the general outside public.

His inspiration had come quite by chance. A fairy story in a magazine had taken a hold on his imagination.

It was the story of a fortunate Princess who had always had everything she wanted. Did she express a wish? It was instantly gratified. A desire? It was granted. She had a devoted father and mother, great riches, beautiful clothes and jewels, slaves to wait upon her and fulfil her lightest whim, laughing maidens to bear her company, all that the heart of a Princess could desire. The handsomest and richest Princes paid her court and sued in vain for her hand, and were willing to kill any number of dragons to prove their devotion. And yet, the loneliness of the Princess was greater than that of the poorest beggar in the land.

He read no more. The ultimate fate of the Princess interested him not at all. A picture had risen up before him of the pleasure-laden Princess with the sad, solitary soul, surfeited with happiness, suffocated with luxury, starving in the Palace of Plenty.

He began painting with furious energy. The fierce joy of creation possessed him.

He represented the Princess surrounded by her court, reclining on a divan. A riot of Eastern color pervaded the picture. The Princess wore a marvelous gown of strange-colored embroideries; her golden hair fell round her, and on her head was a heavy jeweled circlet. Her maidens surrounded her, and Princes knelt at her feet bearing rich gifts. The whole scene was one of luxury and richness.

But the face of the Princess was turned away; she was oblivious of the laughter and mirth around her. Her gaze was fixed on a dark and shadowy corner where stood a seemingly incongruous object: a little grey stone idol with its head buried in its hand in a quaint abandonment of despair.

Was it so incongruous? The eyes of the young Princess rested on it with a strange sympathy, as though a dawning sense of her own isolation drew her glance irresistibly. They were akin, these two. The world was at her feet — yet she was alone: a Lonely Princess looking at a lonely little god.

All London talked of this picture, and

Greta wrote a few hurried words of congratulation from Yorkshire, and Tom Hurley's wife besought Frank Oliver to "come for a weekend and meet a really delightful girl, a great admirer of your work." Frank Oliver laughed once sardonically, and threw the letter into the fire. Success had come — but what was the use of it? He only wanted one thing — that little lonely lady who had gone out of his life forever.

It was Ascot Cup Day, and the policeman on duty in a certain section of the British Museum rubbed his eyes and wondered if he were dreaming, for one does not expect to see there an Ascot vision, in a lace frock and a marvelous hat, a veritable nymph as imagined by a Parisian genius. The policeman stared in rapturous admiration.

The lonely god was not perhaps so surprised. He may have been in his way a powerful little god; at any rate, here was one worshipper brought back to the fold.

The Little Lonely Lady was staring up at him, and her lips moved in a rapid whisper.

"Dear little god, oh! dear little god, please help me! Oh, please do help me!"

Perhaps the little god was flattered. Perhaps, if he was indeed the ferocious, unappeasable deity Frank Oliver had imagined him, the long weary years and the march of civilization had softened his cold, stone heart. Perhaps the Lonely Lady had been right all along and he was really a kind little god. Perhaps it was merely a coincidence. However that may be, it was at that very moment that Frank Oliver walked slowly and sadly through the door of the Assyrian room.

He raised his head and saw the Parisian nymph.

In another moment his arm was round her, and she was stammering out rapid, broken words.

"I was so lonely — *you* know, you must have read that story I wrote; you couldn't have painted that picture unless you had, and unless you had understood. The Princess was I; I had everything, and yet I was lonely beyond words. One day I was going to a fortune-teller's, and I borrowed my maid's clothes. I came in here on the way and saw you looking at the little god. That's how it all began. I pretended — oh! it was hateful of me, and I went on pretending, and afterwards I didn't dare confess that I had told you such dreadful lies. I thought you would be disgusted at the way I had deceived you. I couldn't bear for you to find out, so I went away. Then I wrote that story, and yesterday I saw your picture. It *was* your picture, wasn't it?"

Only the gods really know the word "ingratitude." It is to be presumed that the lonely little god knew the black ingratitude of human nature. As a divinity he had unique opportunities of observing it, yet in the hour of trial, he who had had sacrifices innumerable offered to him, made sacrifice in his turn. He sacrificed his only two worshippers in a strange land, and it showed him to be a great little god in his way, since he sacrificed all that he had.

Through the chinks in his fingers he watched them go, hand in hand, without a backward glance, two happy people who had found heaven and had no need of him any longer.

What was he, after all, but a very lonely little god in a strange land?

VI

Manx Gold

Foreword

"Manx Gold" is no ordinary detective story; indeed, it is probably unique. The detectives are conventional enough, but although they are confronted with a particularly brutal murder, the murderer's identity is not their main concern. They are more interested in unraveling a series of clues to the where-abouts of hidden treasure, a treasure whose existence is not confined to the printed page. Clearly, some explanation is required. . . .

In the winter of 1929, Alderman Arthur B. Crookall had an idea. Crookall was the chairman of the "June Effort," a committee responsible for boosting tourism to the Isle of Man, a small island off the northwest coast of England. His idea was that there should be a treasure hunt, inspired by the many legends of Manx smugglers and their long-forgotten hoards of booty. There would be "real" treasure, hidden about the island, and clues to its location concealed in the framework of a detective story. Some reservations were expressed by members of the committee, but eventually planning began for the "Isle of Man Treasure Hunt Scheme," to take place at the start of the holiday season and run at the same time as a number of other annual events, such as the "Crowning of the Rose Queen" and the midnight yacht race.

But Crookall had to find someone to write the story on which the hunt would be based. Who better than Agatha Christie? Perhaps surprisingly, and for a fee of only sixty pounds, Christie accepted this, her most unusual commission. She visited the Isle of Man at the end of April 1930, staying as the guest of the lieutenant governor, before returning to Devon, where her daughter was ill. During her visit, Christie and Crookall spent several days discussing the treasure hunt, and visited various sites in order to decide where the treasure should be hidden and how the clues should be composed.

The resulting story, "Manx Gold," was published in five installments towards the end of May in the *Daily Dispatch*, a Manchester newspaper. A quarter of a million copies of the story also were distributed in booklet form to guesthouses and hotels across the island. The five clues were published separately, and as the date on which the first was due to appear in the *Dispatch* drew nearer, the June Effort Committee appealed to everyone to "cooperate in order to obtain as much publicity as possible" for the hunt. More tourists meant more tourist revenue, and the hunt was also drawn to the attention of several hundred "Homecomers" who had emigrated from the island to the United States and were due to return as honored guests in June. In the words of the publicity at the time, it was "an opportunity for all Amateur Detectives to test their skill!"

In the story, Juan Faraker and Fenella Mylecharane set out to find four chests of treasure, which have been hidden on the island by their eccentric Uncle Myles. To compete with Juan and Fenella, the reader was advised — like them — to equip himself with "several excellent maps . . . various guidebooks descriptive of the island . . . a book on folklore [and] a book on the history of the island."

The solutions to the clues are given at the end of the story.

Old Mylecharane liv'd up on the broo,
Where Jurby slopes down to the wold,
His croft was all golden with cushag and furze,
His daughter was fair to behold.

"O father, they say you've plenty of store,
But hidden all out of the way
No gold can I see, but its glint on the gorse;
Then what have you done with it, pray?"

"My gold is locked up in a coffer of oak,
Which I dropped in the tide and it sank,
And there it lies fixed like an anchor of hope,
All bright and as safe as the bank."

"I like that song," I said appreciatively as Fenella finished.

"You should do," said Fenella. "It's about our ancestor, yours and mine. Uncle Myles's grandfather. He made a fortune out of smuggling and hid it somewhere, and no one ever knew where."

Ancestry is Fenella's strong point. She takes an interest in all her forbears. My tendencies are strictly modern. The difficult present and the uncertain future absorb all my energy. But I like hearing Fenella singing old Manx ballads.

Fenella is very charming. She is my first cousin and also, from time to time, my fiancée. In moods of financial optimism we are engaged. When a corresponding wave of pessimism sweeps over us and we realize that we shall not be able to marry for at least ten years, we break it off.

"Didn't anyone ever try to find the treasure?" I inquired.

"Of course. But they never did."

"Perhaps they didn't look scientifically."

"Uncle Myles had a jolly good try," said Fenella. "He said anyone with intelligence ought to be able to solve a little problem like that."

That sounded to me very like our Uncle Myles, a cranky and eccentric old gentleman, who lived in the Isle of Man and who was much given to didactic pronouncements.

It was at that moment that the post came — and the letter!

"Good Heavens," cried Fenella. "Talk of the devil — I mean angels — Uncle Myles is dead!"

Both she and I had seen our eccentric relative on only two occasions, so we could neither of us pretend to a very deep grief. The letter was from a firm of lawyers in Douglas, and it informed us that under the will of Mr. Myles Mylecharane, deceased, Fenella and I were joint inheritors of his estate, which consisted of a house near Douglas and an infinitesimal income. Enclosed was a sealed envelope, which Mr. Mylecharane had directed should be forwarded to Fenella at his death. This letter we opened and read its surprising contents. I reproduce it in full, since it was a truly characteristic document.

My dear Fenella and Juan — for I take it that where one of you is the other will not be far away! Or so gossip has whispered.

You may remember having heard me say that anyone displaying a little intelligence could easily find the treasure concealed by my amiable scoundrel of a grandfather. I displayed that intelligence — and my reward was four chests of solid gold — quite like a fairy story, is it not?

Of living relations I have only four: you two, my nephew Ewan Corjeag, whom I have always heard is a thoroughly bad lot, and a cousin, a Doctor Fayll, of whom I have heard very little, and that little not always good.

My estate proper I am leaving to you and Fenella, but I feel a certain obligation laid upon me with regard to this "treasure" which has fallen to my lot solely through my own ingenuity. My amiable ancestor would not, I feel, be satisfied for me to pass it on tamely by inheritance. So I, in my turn, have devised a little problem.

There are still four "chests" of treasure (though in a more modern form than gold ingots or coins) and there are to be four competitors — my four living relations. It would be fairest to assign one "chest" to each — but the world, my children, is not fair. The race is to the swiftest — and often to the most unscrupulous!

Who am I to go against Nature? You must pit your wits against the other two. There will be, I fear, very little chance for you. Goodness and innocence are seldom rewarded in this world. So strongly do I feel this that I have deliberately cheated (unfairness again, you notice!). This letter goes to you twenty-four hours in advance of the letters to the other two. Thus you will have a very good chance of securing the first "treasure" — twenty-four hours' start, if you have any brains at all, ought to be sufficient.

The clues for finding this treasure are to be found at my house in Douglas. The clues for the second "treasure" will not be *released till the first treasure is found. In the second and succeeding cases, therefore, you will all start even. You have my good wishes for success, and nothing would please me better than for you to acquire all four "chests," but for the reasons which I have already stated I think that most unlikely. Remember that no scruples will stand in dear Ewan's way. Do not make the mistake of trusting him in any respect. As to Dr. Richard Fayll, I know little about him, but he is, I fancy, a dark horse.*

Good luck to you both, but with little hopes of your success,

Your affectionate uncle,
Myles Mylecharane

As we reached the signature, Fenella made a leap from my side.

"What is it?" I cried.

Fenella was rapidly turning the pages of an ABC.

"We must get to the Isle of Man as soon as possible," she cried. "How dare he say we were good and innocent and stupid? I'll show him! Juan, we're going to find all four of these 'chests' and get married and live happily ever afterwards, with Rolls-Royces and footmen and marble baths. But we *must* get to the Isle of Man at once."

It was twenty-four hours later. We had arrived in Douglas, interviewed the lawyers, and were now at Maughold House facing Mrs. Skillicorn, our late uncle's house-keeper, a somewhat formidable woman who nevertheless relented a little before Fenella's eagerness.

"Queer ways he had," she said. "Liked to set everyone puzzling and contriving."

"But the clues," cried Fenella. "The clues?"

Deliberately, as she did everything, Mrs. Skillicorn left the room. She returned after an absence of some minutes and held out a folded piece of paper.

We unfolded it eagerly. It contained a dog-gerel rhyme in my uncle's crabbed handwriting.

Four points of the compass so there be
S and W, N and E.
East winds are bad for man and beast.
Go south and west and
North not east.

"Oh!" said Fenella blankly.

"Oh!" said I, with much the same intonation.

Mrs. Skillicorn smiled on us with gloomy relish.

"Not much sense to it, is there?" she said helpfully.

"It — I don't see how to begin," said Fenella, piteously.

"Beginning," I said, with a cheerfulness I did not feel, "is always the difficulty. Once we get going —"

Mrs. Skillicorn smiled more grimly than ever. She was a depressing woman.

"Can't you help us?" asked Fenella coaxingly.

"I know nothing about the silly business. Didn't confide in me, your uncle didn't. I told him to put his money in the bank, and no nonsense. I never knew what he was up to."

"He never went out with any chests — or anything of that kind?"

"That he didn't."

"You don't know when he hid the stuff — whether it was lately or long ago?"

Mrs. Skillicorn shook her head.

"Well," I said, trying to rally. "There are two possibilities. Either the treasure is hidden here, in the actual grounds, or else it may be hidden anywhere on the island. It depends on the bulk, of course."

A sudden brain wave occurred to Fenella.

"You haven't noticed anything missing?" she said. "Among my uncle's things, I mean."

"Why, now, it's odd your saying that —"

"You have, then?"

"As I say, it's odd your saying that. Snuff-boxes — there's at least four of them I can't lay my hand on anywhere."

"Four of them!" cried Fenella. "That must be it! We're on the track. Let's go out in the garden and look about."

"There's nothing there," said Mrs. Skilli-corn. "I'd know if there were. Your uncle couldn't have buried anything in the garden without my knowing about it."

"Points of the compass are mentioned," I said. "The first thing we need is a map of the island."

"There's one on that desk," said Mrs. Skil-licorn.

Fenella unfolded it eagerly. Something fluttered out as she did so. I caught it.

"Hullo," I said. "This looks like a further clue."

We both went over it eagerly.

It appeared to be a rude kind of map. There was a cross on it and a circle and a pointing arrow, and directions were roughly indicated, but it was hardly illuminating. We studied it in silence.

"It's not very illuminating, is it?" said Fenella.

"Naturally it wants puzzling over," I said. "We can't expect it to leap to the eye."

Mrs. Skillicorn interrupted with a suggestion of supper, to which we agreed thankfully.

"And could we have some coffee?" said Fenella. "Lots of it — very black."

Mrs. Skillicorn provided us with an excellent meal, and at its conclusion a large jug of coffee made its appearance.

"And now," said Fenella, "we must get down to it."

"The first thing," I said, "is direction. This seems to point clearly to the northeast of the island."

"It seems so. Let's look at the map."

We studied the map attentively.

"It all depends on how you take the thing," said Fenella. "Does the cross represent the treasure? Or is it something like a church? There really ought to be rules!"

"That would make it too easy."

"I suppose it would. Why are there little lines on one side of the circle and not the other?"

"I don't know."

"Are there any more maps anywhere?"

We were sitting in the library. There were several excellent maps. There were also various guidebooks descriptive of the island.

There was a book on folklore. There was a book on the history of the island. We read them all.

And at last we formed a possible theory.

"It does seem to fit," said Fenella at last. "I mean the two together is a likely conjunction which doesn't seem to occur anywhere else."

"It's worth trying, anyhow," I said. "I don't think we can do anything more to-night. Tomorrow, first thing, we'll hire a car and go off and try our luck."

"It's tomorrow now," said Fenella. "Half past two! Just fancy!!"

Early morning saw us on the road. We had hired a car for a week, arranging to drive it ourselves. Fenella's spirits rose as we sped along the excellent road, mile after mile.

"If only it wasn't for the other two, what fun this would be," she said. "This is where the Derby was originally run, wasn't it? Before it was changed to Epsom. How queer that is to think of!"

I drew her attention to a farmhouse.

"That must be where there is said to be a secret passage running under the sea to that island."

"What fun! I love secret passages, don't you? Oh! Juan, we're getting quite near now. I'm terribly excited. If we should be right!"

Five minutes later we abandoned the car.

"Everything's in the right position," said Fenella tremulously.

We walked on.

"Six of them — that's right. Now between these two. Have you got the compass?"

Five minutes later, we were standing facing each other, an incredulous joy on our faces — and on my outstretched palm lay an antique snuffbox.

We had been successful!

On our return to Maughold House, Mrs. Skillicorn met us with the information that two gentlemen had arrived. One had departed again, but the other was in the library.

A tall, fair man with a florid face rose smilingly from an armchair as we entered the room.

"Mr. Faraker and Miss Mylecharane? Delighted to meet you. I am your distant cousin, Dr. Fayll. Amusing game, all this, isn't it?"

His manner was urbane and pleasant, but I took an immediate dislike to him. I felt that in some way the man was dangerous. His pleasant manner was, somehow, too pleasant, and his eyes never met yours fairly.

"I'm afraid we've got bad news for you," I said. "Miss Mylecharane and myself have already discovered the first 'treasure.'"

He took it very well.

"Too bad — too bad. Posts from here must be odd. Barford and I started at once."

We did not dare to confess the perfidy of Uncle Myles.

"Anyway, we shall all start fair for the second round," said Fenella.

"Splendid. What about getting down to the clues right away? Your excellent Mrs. — er — Skillicorn holds them, I believe?"

"That wouldn't be fair to Mr. Corjeag," said Fenella, quickly. "We must wait for him."

"True, true — I had forgotten. We must get in touch with him as quickly as possible. I will see to that — you two must be tired out and want to rest."

Thereupon he took his departure. Ewan Corjeag must have been unexpectedly difficult to find, for it was not till nearly eleven o'clock that night that Dr. Fayll rang up. He suggested that he and Ewan should come over to Maughold House at ten o'clock the following morning, when Mrs. Skillicorn could hand us out the clues.

"That will do splendidly," said Fenella. "Ten o'clock tomorrow."

We retired to bed tired but happy.

The following morning we were aroused

by Mrs. Skillicorn, completely shaken out of her usual pessimistic calm.

"Whatever do you think?" she panted. "The house has been broken into."

"Burglars?" I exclaimed incredulously. "Has anything been taken?"

"Not a thing — and that's the odd part of it! No doubt they were after the silver — but the door being locked on the outside they couldn't get any further."

Fenella and I accompanied her to the scene of the outrage, which happened to be in her own sitting room. The window there had undeniably been forced, yet nothing seemed to have been taken. It was all rather curious.

"I don't see what they can have been looking for," said Fenella.

"It's not as though there were a 'treasure chest' hidden in the house," I agreed facetiously. Suddenly an idea flashed into my mind. I turned to Mrs. Skillicorn. "The clues — the clues you were to give us this morning?"

"Why to be sure — they're in that top drawer." She went across to it. "Why — I do declare — there's nothing here! They're gone!"

"Not burglars," I said. "Our esteemed relations!" And I remembered Uncle Myles's warning on the subject of unscrupulous dealing. Clearly he had known what he was talking about. A dirty trick!

"Hush," said Fenella suddenly, holding up a finger. "What was that?"

The sound she had caught came plainly to our ears. It was a groan and it came from outside. We went to the window and leaned out. There was shrubbery growing against this side of the house and we could see nothing; but the groan came again, and we could see that the bushes seemed to have been disturbed and trampled.

We hurried down and out round the house. The first thing we found was a fallen ladder, showing how the thieves had reached the window. A few steps further brought us to where a man was lying.

He was a youngish man, dark, and he was evidently badly injured, for his head was lying in a pool of blood. I knelt down beside him.

"We must get a doctor at once. I'm afraid he's dying."

The gardener was sent off hurriedly. I slipped my hand into his breast pocket and brought out a pocket book. On it were the initials E. C.

"Ewan Corjeag," said Fenella.

The man's eyes opened. He said faintly: "Fell from ladder . . ." then lost consciousness again.

Close by his head was a large jagged stone stained with blood.

"It's clear enough," I said. "The ladder slipped and he fell, striking his head on this stone. I'm afraid it's done for him, poor fellow."

"So you think that was it?" said Fenella, in an odd tone of voice.

But at that moment the doctor arrived. He held out little hope of recovery. Ewan Corjeag was moved into the house and a nurse was sent for to take charge of him. Nothing could be done, and he would die a couple of hours later.

We had been sent for and were standing by his bed. His eyes opened and flickered.

"We are your cousins Juan and Fenella," I said. "Is there anything we can do?"

He made a faint negative motion of the head. A whisper came from his lips. I bent to catch it.

"Do you want the clue? I'm done. Don't let Fayll do you down."

"Yes," said Fenella. "Tell me."

Something like a grin came over his face.

"D'ye ken —" he began.

Then suddenly his head fell over sideways and he died.

"I don't like it," said Fenella suddenly.

"What don't you like?"

"Listen, Juan. Ewan stole those clues — he admits falling from the ladder. *Then where are they?* We've seen all the contents of his pockets. There were three sealed envelopes, so Mrs. Skillicorn says. Those sealed envelopes aren't there."

"What do you think, then?"

"I think there was someone else there, someone who jerked away the ladder so that Ewan fell. And that stone — he never fell on it — it was brought from some distance away — I've found the mark. He was deliberately bashed on the head with it."

"But Fenella — that's murder!"

"Yes," said Fenella, very white. "It's murder. Remember, Dr. Fayll never turned up at ten o'clock this morning. Where is he?"

"You think he's the murderer?"

"Yes. You know — this treasure — it's a lot of money, Juan."

"And we've no idea where to look for him," I said. "A pity Corjeag couldn't have finished what he was going to say."

"There's one thing that might help. This was in his hand."

She handed me a torn snapshot.

"Suppose it's a clue. The murderer snatched it away and never noticed he'd left

133

a corner of it behind. If we were to find the other half —"

"To do that," I said, "we must find the second treasure. Let's look at this thing."

"Hmm," I said, "there's nothing much to go by. That seems a kind of tower in the middle of the circle, but it would be very hard to identify."

Fenella nodded.

"Dr. Fayll has the important half. He knows where to look. We've got to find that man, Juan, and watch him. Of course, we won't let him see we suspect."

"I wonder whereabouts in the island he is this minute. If we only knew —"

My mind went back to the dying man. Suddenly I sat up excitedly.

"Fenella," I said, "Corjeag wasn't Scotch?"

"No, of course not."

"Well, then, don't you see? What he meant, I mean?"

"No?"

I scribbled something on a piece of paper and tossed it to her.

"What's this?"

"The name of a firm that might help us."

"Bellman and True. Who are they? Lawyers?"

"No — they're more in our line — private detectives."

134

And I proceeded to explain.

"Dr. Fayll to see you," said Mrs. Skillicorn.

We looked at each other. Twenty-four hours had elapsed. We had returned from our quest successful for the second time. Not wishing to draw attention to ourselves, we had journeyed in the Snaefell — a charabanc.

"I wonder if he knows we saw him in the distance?" murmured Fenella.

"It's extraordinary. If it hadn't been for the hint that photograph gave us —"

"Hush — and do be careful, Juan. He must be simply furious at our having outwitted him in spite of everything."

No trace of it appeared in the doctor's manner, however. He entered the room his urbane and charming self, and I felt my faith in Fenella's theory dwindling.

"What a shocking tragedy!" he said. "Poor Corjeag. I suppose he was — well — trying to steal a march on us. Retribution was swift. Well, well — we scarcely knew him, poor fellow. You must have wondered why I didn't turn up this morning as arranged. I got a fake message — Corjeag's doing, I suppose — it sent me off on a wild-goose chase right across the island. And now you two have romped home again. How do you do it?"

There was a note of really eager inquiry in his voice which did not escape me.

"Cousin Ewan was fortunately able to speak just before he died," said Fenella.

I was watching the man, and I could swear I saw alarm leap into his eyes at her words.

"Eh — eh? What's that?" he said.

"He was just able to give us a clue as to the whereabouts of the treasure," explained Fenella.

"Oh! I see — I see. I've been clean out of things — though, curiously enough, I myself was in that part of the island. You may have seen me strolling round."

"We were so busy," said Fenella apologetically.

"Of course, of course. You must have run across the thing more or less by accident. Lucky young people, aren't you? Well, what's the next program? Will Mrs. Skillicorn oblige us with the new clues?"

But it seemed that this third set of clues had been deposited with the lawyer, and we all three repaired to the lawyer's office, where the sealed envelopes were handed over to us.

The contents were simple. A map with a certain area marked off on it, and a paper of directions attached.

In '85, this place made history.
Ten paces from the landmark to
The east, then an equal ten
Paces north. Stand there
Looking east. Two trees are in the
Line of vision. One of them
Was sacred in this island. Draw
A circle five feet from
The Spanish chestnut and,
With head bent, walk round. Look well.
You'll find.

"Looks as though we are going to tread on each other's toes a bit today," commented the doctor.

True to my policy of apparent friendliness, I offered him a lift in our car, which he accepted. We had lunch at Port Erin, and then started on our search.

I had debated in my own mind the reason of my uncle's depositing this particular set of clues with his lawyer. Had he foreseen the possibility of a theft? And had he determined that not more than one set of clues should fall into the thief's possession?

The treasure hunt this afternoon was not without its humor. The area of search was limited and we were continually in sight of each other. We eyed each other suspiciously, each trying to determine whether the other

137

was further on or had had a brain wave.

"This is all part of Uncle Myles's plan," said Fenella. "He wanted us to watch each other and go through all the agonies of thinking the other person was getting there."

"Come," I said. "Let's get down to it scientifically. We've got one definite clue to start on. *In '85 this place made history.*' Look up the reference books we've got with us and see if we can't hunt that down. Once we get that —"

"He's looking in that hedge," interrupted Fenella. "Oh! I can't bear it. If he's got it —"

"Attend to me," I said firmly. "There's really only one way to go about it — the proper way."

"There are so few trees on the island that it would be much simpler just to look for a chestnut tree!" said Fenella.

I pass over the next hour. We grew hot and despondent — and all the time we were tortured with fear that Fayll might be succeeding whilst we failed.

"I remember once reading in a detective story," I said, "how a fellow stuck a paper of writing in a bath of acid — and all sorts of other words came out."

"Do you think — but we haven't got a bath of acid!"

"I don't think Uncle Myles could expect

138

expert chemical knowledge. But there's common or garden heat —"

We slipped round the corner of a hedge and in a minute or two I had kindled a few twigs. I held the paper as close to the blaze as I dared. Almost at once I was rewarded by seeing characters begin to appear at the foot of the sheet. There were just two words.

"Kirkhill Station," read out Fenella.

Just at that moment Fayll came round the corner. Whether he had heard or not we had no means of judging. He showed nothing.

"But Juan," said Fenella, when he moved away, "there isn't a Kirkhill Station!" She held out the map as she spoke.

"No," I said examining it, "but look here."

And with a pencil I drew a line on it.

"Of course! And somewhere on that line —"

"Exactly."

"But I wish we knew the exact spot."

It was then that my second brain wave came to me.

"We do!" I cried, and seizing the pencil again, I said: "Look!"

Fenella uttered a cry.

"How idiotic!" she cried. "And how marvelous: What a sell! Really. Uncle Myles was a most ingenious old gentleman!"

The time had come for the last clue. This, the lawyer had informed us, was not in his keeping. It was to be posted to us on receipt of a postcard sent by him. He would impart no further information.

Nothing arrived, however, on the morning it should have done, and Fenella and I went through agonies, believing that Fayll had managed somehow to intercept our letter. The next day, however, our fears were calmed and the mystery explained when we received the following illiterate scrawl:

Dear Sir or Madam,
Escuse delay but have been all sixes and sevens but i do now as mr. Mylecharane axed me to and send you the piece of riting wot as been in my family many long years the wot he wanted it for i do not know.
thanking you i am
Mary Kerruish

"Postmark-Bride," I remarked. "Now for the 'piece of riting handed down in my family'!"

Upon a rock, a sign you'll see.
O, tell me what the point of
That may be? Well, firstly,(A). Near

140

By you'll find, quite suddenly, the light
You seek. Then (B). A house. A
Cottage with a thatch and wall.
A meandering lane near by. That's all.

"It's very unfair to begin with a rock," said Fenella. "There are rocks everywhere. How can you tell which one has the sign on it?"

"If we could settle on the district," I said, "it ought to be fairly easy to find the rock. It must have a mark on it pointing in a certain direction, and in that direction there will be something hidden which will throw light on the finding of the treasure."

"I think you're right," said Fenella.

"That's A. The new clue will give us a hint where B, the cottage, is to be found. The treasure itself is hidden down a lane alongside the cottage. But clearly we've got to find A first."

Owing to the difficulty of the initial step, Uncle Myles's last problem proved a real teaser. To Fenella falls the distinction of unraveling it — and even then she did not accomplish it for nearly a week. Now and then we had come across Fayll in our search of rocky districts, but the area was a wide one.

When we finally made our discovery it was late in the evening. Too late, I said, to start off to the place indicated. Fenella disagreed.

"Supposing Fayll finds it, too," she said. "And we wait till tomorrow and he starts off tonight. How we should kick ourselves!"

Suddenly, a marvelous idea occurred to me.

"Fenella," I said, "do you still believe that Fayll murdered Ewan Corjeag?"

"I do."

"Then I think that now we've got our chance to bring the crime home to him."

"That man makes me shiver. He's bad all through. Tell me."

"Advertize the fact that we've found A. Then start off. Ten to one he'll follow us. It's a lonely place — just what would suit his book. He'll come out in the open if we pretend to find the treasure."

"And then?"

"And then," I said, "he'll have a little surprise."

It was close on midnight. We had left the car some distance away and were creeping along by the side of a wall. Fenella had a powerful flashlight which she was using. I myself carried a revolver. I was taking no chances.

Suddenly, with a low cry, Fenella stopped.

142

"Look, Juan," she cried. "We've got it. At last."

For a moment I was off my guard. Led by instinct I whirled round — but too late. Fayll stood six paces away and his revolver covered us both.

"Good evening," he said. "This trick is mine. You'll hand over that treasure, if you please."

"Would you like me also to hand over something else?" I asked. "Half a snapshot torn from a dying man's hand? *You have the other half, I think.*"

His hand wavered.

"What are you talking about?" he growled.

"The truth's known," I said. "You and Corjeag were there together. You pulled away the ladder and crashed his head with that stone. The police are cleverer than you imagine, Dr. Fayll."

"They know, do they? Then, by Heaven, I'll swing for three murders instead of one!"

"Drop, Fenella," I screamed. And at the same minute his revolver barked loudly.

We had both dropped in the heather, and before he could fire again uniformed men sprang out from behind the wall where they had been hiding. A moment later Fayll had been handcuffed and led away.

I caught Fenella in my arms.

"I knew I was right," she said tremulously.

"Darling!" I cried, "it was too risky. He might have shot you."

"But he didn't," said Fenella. "And we know where the treasure is."

"Do we?"

"I do. See" — she scribbled a word. "We'll look for it tomorrow. There can't be many hiding places there, I should say."

It was just noon when:

"Eureka!" said Fenella softly. "The fourth snuffbox! We've got them all. Uncle Myles would be pleased. And now —"

"Now," I said, "we can be married and live together happily ever afterwards."

"We'll live in the Isle of Man," said Fenella.

"On Manx Gold," I said, and laughed aloud for sheer happiness.

Afterword

The treasure is all that is left of the lost fortune of "Old Mylecharane," a legendary Manx smuggler. In reality, the treasure took the form of four snuffboxes, each about the size of a matchbox and containing an eighteenth-century Manx halfpenny with a hole in it, through which was tied a length of colored ribbon, and a neatly folded document, executed with many flourishes in India ink and signed by Alderman Crookall, which directed the finder to report at once to the clerk at the town hall in Douglas, the capital of the Isle of Man. Finders were instructed to take with them the snuffbox and its contents in order to claim a prize of one hundred pounds (equivalent to about three thousand pounds today). They also had to bring with them proof of identity, for only visitors to the island were allowed to search for the treasure; Manx residents were excluded from the hunt.

A Little Intelligence
Could Easily Find the Treasure

The sole purpose of the first clue in "Manx Gold," the rhyme which begins "Four points of the compass so there be," published in the *Daily Dispatch* on Saturday, May 31, was to indicate that the four treasures would be found in the north, south, and west of the island, but not in the east. The clue to the location of the first snuffbox was in fact the second clue, a map published on June 7. However, the treasure had already been found by a tailor from Inverness, William

Shaw, because sufficient clues to its location were contained in the story itself.

The most important clue was Fenella's remark that the hiding place was near the place "where Derby was originally run . . . before it was changed to Epsom." This is a reference to the famous English horse race, which was first run at Derbyhaven in the southeast of the Isle of Man. The "quite near" island to which "a secret passage" was rumored to run from a farmhouse can easily be identified as St. Michael's Isle, on which, in addition to the twelfth-century chapel of St. Michael, is a circular stone tower known as the Derby Fort, from which the island gets its alternative name, Fort Island — "the two together is a likely conjunction which doesn't seem to occur anywhere else." The fort was represented on the map by a circle with six lines projected from it to represent the six historical cannons — "six of them" — in the fort; the chapel was represented by a cross.

The small pewter snuffbox was hidden on a rocky ledge running in a northeasterly direction from between the middle two cannons — "between these two have you got the compass?" — while Juan's initial suggestion that the clue "points to the northeast of the island" was a red herring.

Too Easy

The second snuffbox, apparently constructed from horn, was located on June 9 by Richard Highton, a Lancashire builder. As Fenella made clear to the murderous Dr. Fayll, Ewan Corjeag's dying words, "D'ye ken —" are a clue to the whereabouts of the treasure. In fact, they are the opening words of the traditional English song "John Peel," about a Cumbrian huntsman, and when Juan suggested that "Bellman and True" was the "name of a firm that might help us," he was not referring to the "firm of lawyers in Douglas" mentioned at the beginning of the story but to two of John Peel's hounds, as named in the song. With these clues, the subject of the "torn snapshot," which was published as the third clue on June 9, would not have been "very hard to identify"; it was the ruins of the fourteenth-century Peel Castle on St. Patrick's Isle, and curved lines along the photograph's left-hand edge were the curlicues on the arm of a bench on Peel Hill, which looks down on the castle and under which the snuffbox was hidden. The charabanc journey to Snaefell, the highest peak on the Isle of Man, was another red herring.

The third "treasure" was found by Mr. Herbert Elliot, a Manx-born ship's engineer living in Liverpool. Mr. Elliot later claimed that he had not read "Manx Gold" nor even studied the clues, but had simply decided on a likely area where, very early on the morning of July 8, he chanced upon the snuffbox, hidden in a gully.

The principal clue to its whereabouts was hidden in the fourth clue, published on June 14 (the verse beginning "In '85, this place made history"), in which the second word of each line spells out the following message: "85 . . . paces . . . east . . . north . . . east . . . of . . . sacred . . . circle . . . Spanish . . . head." The "sacred circle" is the Meayll circle on Mull Hill, a megalithic monument a little over a mile from the Spanish Head, the most southerly point of the island. The reference to an important event "in '85" and a Spanish chestnut, which from contemporary accounts proved a diversion for many searchers, were false leads. As for "Kirkhill Station," the clue uncovered by Juan, Fenella rightly said that there was no such place. However, there is a village called Kirkhill and there is also a railway station at Port Erin, where Juan and Fenella had had lunch before starting their search. If a line is drawn from Kirkhill to Port Erin and continued southward, it eventually crosses the Meayll circle, "the exact spot" identified by Juan.

A Real Teaser

Unfortunately, as was the case with the clues to the location of the third snuffbox, those for the fourth were never solved. The fifth and final clue, the verse beginning "Upon a rock, a sign you'll see," was published on June 21, but on July 10, at the end of the extended period allowed for the hunt, which had originally been intended to finish at the end of June, the final "treasure" was "lifted" by the Mayor of Douglas. Two days later, as a "sequel" to the story, the *Daily Dispatch* published a photograph of the event and Christie's explanation of the final clue:

> *That last clue still makes me smile when I remember the time we wasted looking for rocks with a sign on them. The real clue was so simple — the words "sixes and sevens" in the covering letter.*
>
> *Take the sixth and seventh words of each line of the verse, and you get this:* "You'll see. Point of (A). Near the lighthouse a wall." *See the point of (A) we identified*

as the Point of Ayre. We spent some time finding the right wall, and the treasure itself was not there. Instead, there were four figures — 2, 5, 6, and 9 scrawled on a stone.

Apply them to the letters of the first line of the verse, and you get the word "park." There is only one real park in the Isle of Man, at Ramsey. We searched that park, and found at last what we sought.

The thatched building in question was a small refreshment kiosk, and the path leading past it ran up to an ivy-covered wall, which was the hiding place of the elusive snuffbox. The fact that the letter had been posted in Bride was an additional clue, as this village is near the lighthouse at the Point of Ayre, the northernmost tip of the island.

It is impossible to judge whether or not "Manx Gold" was a successful means of promoting tourism on the Isle of Man. Certainly, it appears that there were more visitors in 1930 than in previous years, but how far that increase could be ascribed to the treasure hunt is far from clear. Contemporary press reports show that there were many who doubted that it had been of any real value, and at a civic lunch to mark the end of the hunt, Alderman Crookall responded to a vote of thanks by railing against those who had failed to talk up the hunt — they were "slackers and grousers who never did anything but offer up criticism."

The fact that they were not allowed to take part in the hunt might have been a cause of apathy among the islanders, even though the *Daily Dispatch* offered the Manx resident with whom each finder was staying a prize of five guineas, equivalent to about one hundred fifty pounds today. This also might have accounted for various acts of gentle "sabotage," such as the laying of false snuffboxes and spoof clues, including a rock on which the word "lift" was painted but under which was nothing more interesting than discarded fruit peel.

While there never has been any other event quite like the Isle of Man treasure hunt, Agatha Christie *did* go on to write mysteries with a similar theme. Most obvious of these is the challenge laid down to Charmian Stroud and Edward Rossiter by their eccentric Uncle Mathew in "Strange Jest," a Miss Marple story first published in 1941 as "A Case of Buried Treasure" and collected in *Three Blind Mice* (1948). There is also a similarly structured "murder hunt" in the Poirot novel *Dead Man's Folly* (1956).

VII

Within a Wall

It was Mrs. Lemprière who discovered the existence of Jane Haworth. It would be, of course. Somebody once said that Mrs. Lemprière was easily the most hated woman in London, but that, I think, is an exaggeration. She has certainly a knack of tumbling on the one thing you wish to keep quiet about, and she does it with real genius. It is always an accident.

In this case we had been having tea in Alan Everard's studio. He gave these teas occasionally, and used to stand about in corners, wearing very old clothes, rattling the coppers in his trouser pockets and looking profoundly miserable.

I do not suppose anyone will dispute Everard's claim to genius at this date. His two most famous pictures, *Color* and *The Connoisseur*, which belong to his early period, before he became a fashionable portrait painter, were purchased by the nation last year, and for once the choice went unchallenged. But at the date of which I speak, Everard was only beginning to come into his own, and we were free to consider that we had discovered him.

It was his wife who organized these parties. Everard's attitude to her was a peculiar one. That he adored her was evident, and only to be expected. Adoration was Isobel's due. But he seemed always to feel himself slightly in her debt. He assented to anything she wished, not so much through tenderness as through an unalterable conviction that she had a right to her own way. I suppose that was natural enough, too, when one comes to think of it.

For Isobel Loring had been really very celebrated. When she came out she had been *the* débutante of the season. She had everything except money; beauty, position, breeding, brains. Nobody expected her to marry for love. She wasn't that kind of girl. In her second season she had three strings to her bow, the heir to a dukedom, a rising politician, and a South African millionaire. And then, to everyone's surprise, she married Alan Everard — a struggling young painter whom no one had ever heard of.

It is a tribute to her personality, I think, that everyone went on calling her Isobel Loring. Nobody ever alluded to her as Isobel

Everard. It would be: "I saw Isobel Loring this morning. Yes — with her husband, young Everard, the painter fellow."

People said Isobel had "done for herself." It would, I think, have "done" for most men to be known as "Isobel Loring's husband. But Everard was different. Isobel's talent for success hadn't failed her after all. Alan Everard painted *Color*.

I suppose everyone knows the picture: a stretch of road with a trench dug down it, and turned earth, reddish in color, a shining length of brown glazed drainpipe and the huge navvy, resting for a minute on his spade — a Herculean figure in stained corduroys with a scarlet neckerchief. His eyes look out at you from the canvas, without intelligence, without hope, but with a dumb unconscious pleading, the eyes of a magnificent brute beast. It is a flaming thing — a symphony of orange and red. A lot has been written about its symbolism, about what it is meant to express. Alan Everard himself says he didn't mean it to express anything. He was, he said, nauseated by having had to look at a lot of pictures of Venetian sunsets, and a sudden longing for a riot of purely English color assailed him.

After that, Everard gave the world that epic painting of a public house — *Romance*:

the black street with rain falling — the half-open door, the lights and shining glasses, the little foxy-faced man passing through the doorway, small, mean, insignificant, with lips parted and eyes eager, passing in to forget.

On the strength of these two pictures Everard was acclaimed as a painter of "working men." He had his niche. But he refused to stay in it. His third and most brilliant work, a full-length portrait of Sir Rufus Herschman. The famous scientist is painted against a background of retorts and crucibles and laboratory shelves. The whole has what may be called a Cubist effect, but the lines of perspective run strangely.

And now he had completed his fourth work — a portrait of his wife. We had been invited to see and criticize. Everard himself scowled and looked out of the window; Isobel Loring moved amongst the guests, talking technique with unerring accuracy.

We made comments. We had to. We praised the painting of the pink satin. The treatment of that, we said, was really marvelous. Nobody had painted satin in quite that way before.

Mrs. Lemprière, who is one of the most intelligent art critics I know, took me aside almost at once.

"Georgia," she said, "what has he done to

himself? The thing's dead. It's smooth. It's — oh! it's damnable."

"*Portrait of a Lady in Pink Satin*?" I suggested.

"Exactly. And yet the technique's perfect. And the care! There's enough work there for sixteen pictures."

"Too much work?" I suggested.

"Perhaps that's it. If there ever was anything there, he's killed it. An extremely beautiful woman in a pink satin dress. Why not a colored photograph?"

"Why not?" I agreed. "Do you suppose he knows?"

"Of course he knows," said Mrs. Lemprière scornfully. "Don't you see the man's on edge? It comes, I daresay, of mixing up sentiment and business. He's put his whole soul into painting Isobel, because she is Isobel, and in sparing her, he's lost her. He's been too kind. You've got to — to destroy the flesh before you can get at the soul sometimes."

I nodded reflectively. Sir Rufus Herschman had not been flattered physically, but Everard had succeeded in putting on the canvas a personality that was unforgettable.

"And Isobel's got such a very forceful personality," continued Mrs. Lemprière.

"Perhaps Everard can't paint women," I said.

"Perhaps not," said Mrs. Lemprière thoughtfully. "Yes, that may be the explanation."

And it was then, with her usual genius for accuracy, that she pulled out a canvas that was leaning with its face to the wall. There were about eight of them, stacked carelessly. It was pure chance that Mrs. Lemprière selected the one she did — but as I said before, these things happen with Mrs. Lemprière.

"Ah!" said Mrs. Lemprière as she turned it to the light.

It was unfinished, a mere rough sketch. The woman, or girl — she was not, I thought, more than twenty-five or -six — was leaning forward, her chin on her hand. Two things struck me at once: the extraordinary vitality of the picture and the amazing cruelty of it. Everard had painted with a vindictive brush. The attitude even was a cruel one — it had brought out every awkwardness, every sharp angle, every crudity. It was a study in brown — brown dress, brown background, brown eyes — wistful, eager eyes. Eagerness was, indeed, the prevailing note of it.

Mrs. Lemprière looked at it for some minutes in silence. Then she called to Everard.

"Alan," she said. "Come here. Who's this?"

Everard came over obediently. I saw the sudden flash of annoyance that he could not quite hide.

"That's only a daub," he said. "I don't suppose I shall ever finish it."

"Who is she?" said Mrs. Lemprière.

Everard was clearly unwilling to answer, and his unwillingness was as meat and drink to Mrs. Lemprière, who always believes the worst on principle.

"A friend of mine. A Miss Jane Haworth."

"I've never met her here," said Mrs. Lemprière.

"She doesn't come to these shows." He paused a minute, then added: "She's Winnie's godmother."

Winnie was his little daughter, aged five.

"Really?" said Mrs. Lemprière. "Where does she live?"

"Battersea. A flat."

"Really," said Mrs. Lemprière again, and then added: "And what has she ever done to you?"

"To me?"

"To you. To make you so — ruthless."

"Oh, that!" he laughed. "Well, you know, she's not a beauty. I can't make her one out of friendship, can I?"

"You've done the opposite," said Mrs.

158

Lemprière. "You've caught hold of every defect of hers and exaggerated it and twisted it. You've tried to make her ridiculous — but you haven't succeeded, my child. That portrait, if you finish it, will live."

Everard looked annoyed.

"It's not bad," he said lightly, "for a sketch, that is. But, of course, it's not a patch on Isobel's portrait. That's far and away the best thing I've ever done."

He said the last words defiantly and aggressively. Neither of us answered.

"Far and away the best thing," he repeated.

Some of the others had drawn near us. They, too, caught sight of the sketch. There were exclamations, comments. The atmosphere began to brighten up.

It was in this way that I first heard of Jane Haworth. Later, I was to meet her — twice. I was to hear details of her life from one of her most intimate friends. I was to learn much from Alan Everard himself. Now that they are both dead, I think it is time to contradict some of the stories Mrs. Lemprière is busily spreading abroad. Call some of my story invention if you will — it is not far from the truth.

When the guests had left, Alan Everard

turned the portrait of Jane Haworth with its face to the wall again. Isobel came down the room and stood beside him.

"A success, do you think?" she asked thoughtfully. "Or — not quite a success?"

"The portrait?" he asked quickly.

"No, silly, the party. Of course the portrait's a success."

"It's the best thing I've done," Everard declared aggressively.

"We're getting on," said Isobel. "Lady Charmington wants you to paint her."

"Oh, Lord!" He frowned. "I'm not a fashionable portrait painter, you know."

"You will be. You'll get to the top of the tree."

"That's not the tree I want to get to the top of."

"But, Alan dear, that's the way to make mints of money."

"Who wants mints of money?"

"Perhaps I do," she said smiling.

At once he felt apologetic, ashamed. If she had not married him she could have had her mints of money. And she needed it. A certain amount of luxury was her proper setting.

"We've not done so badly just lately," he said wistfully.

"No, indeed; but the bills are coming in rather fast."

160

Bills — always bills!

He walked up and down.

"Oh, hang it! I don't want to paint Lady Charmington," he burst out, rather like a petulant child.

Isobel smiled a little. She stood by the fire without moving. Alan stopped his restless pacing and came nearer to her. What was there in her, in her stillness, her inertia, that drew him — drew him like a magnet? How beautiful she was — her arms like sculptured white marble, the pure gold of her hair, her lips — red, full lips.

He kissed them — felt them fasten on his own. Did anything else matter? What was there in Isobel that soothed you, that took all your cares from you? She drew you into her own beautiful inertia and held you there, quiet and content. Poppy and mandragora; you drifted there, on a dark lake, asleep.

"I'll do Lady Charmington," he said presently. "What does it matter? I shall be bored — but after all, painters must eat. There's Mr. Pots the painter, Mrs. Pots the painter's wife, and Miss Pots the painter's daughter — all needing sustenance."

"Absurd boy!" said Isobel. "Talking of our daughter — you ought to go and see Jane some time. She was here yesterday, and said she hadn't seen you for months."

"Jane was here?"

"Yes — to see Winnie."

Alan brushed Winnie aside.

"Did she see the picture of you?"

"Yes."

"What did she think of it?"

"She said it was splendid."

"Oh!"

He frowned, lost in thought.

"Mrs. Lemprière suspects you of a guilty passion for Jane, I think," remarked Isobel. "Her nose twitched a good deal."

"That woman!" said Alan, with deep disgust. "That woman! What wouldn't she think? What doesn't she think?"

"Well, *I* don't think," said Isobel, smiling. "So go on and see Jane soon."

Alan looked across at her. She was sitting now on a low couch by the fire. Her face was half turned away, the smile still lingered on her lips. And at that moment he felt bewildered, confused, as though a mist had formed round him, and suddenly parting, had given him a glimpse into a strange country.

Something said to him: "Why does she want you to go and see Jane? There's a reason." Because with Isobel, there was bound to be a reason. There was no impulse in Isobel, only calculation.

"Do you like Jane?" he asked suddenly.

"She's a dear," said Isobel.

"Yes, but do you really like her?"

"Of course. She's so devoted to Winnie. By the way, she wants to carry Winnie off to the seaside next week. You don't mind, do you? It will leave us free for Scotland."

"It will be extraordinarily convenient."

It would, indeed, be just that. Extraordinarily convenient. He looked across at Isobel with a sudden suspicion. Had she *asked* Jane? Jane was so easily imposed upon.

Isobel got up and went out of the room, humming to herself. Oh, well, it didn't matter. Anyway, he would go and see Jane.

Jane Haworth lived at the top of a block of mansion flats overlooking Battersea Park. When Everard had climbed four flights of stairs and pressed the bell, he felt annoyed with Jane. Why couldn't she live somewhere more get-at-able? When, not having obtained an answer, he had pressed the bell three times, his annoyance had grown greater. Why couldn't she keep someone capable of answering the door?

Suddenly it opened, and Jane herself stood in the doorway. She was flushed.

"Where's Alice?" asked Everard, without any attempt at greeting.

"Well, I'm afraid — I mean — she's not well today."

"Drink, you mean?" said Everard grimly.

What a pity that Jane was such an inveterate liar.

"I suppose that's it," said Jane reluctantly.

"Let me see her."

He strode into the flat. Jane followed him with disarming meekness. He found the delinquent Alice in the kitchen. There was no doubt whatever as to her condition. He followed Jane into the sitting room in grim silence.

"You'll have to get rid of that woman," he said. "I told you so before."

"I know you did, Alan, but I can't do that. You forget, her husband's in prison."

"Where he ought to be," said Everard. "How often has that woman been drunk in the three months you've had her?"

"Not so very many times; three or four perhaps. She gets depressed, you know."

"Three or four! Nine or ten would be nearer the mark. How does she cook? Rottenly. Is she the least assistance or comfort to you in this flat? None whatever. For God's sake, get rid of her tomorrow morning and engage a girl who is of some use."

Jane looked at him unhappily.

"You won't," said Everard gloomily, sinking into a big armchair. "You're such an impossibly sentimental creature. What's this

I hear about your taking Winnie to the sea-side? Who suggested it, you or Isobel?"

Jane said very quickly: "I did, of course."

"Jane," said Everard, "if you would only learn to speak the truth, I should be quite fond of you. Sit down, and for goodness sake don't tell any more lies for at least ten minutes."

"Oh, Alan!" said Jane, and sat down.

The painter examined her critically for a minute or two. Mrs. Lemprière — that woman — had been quite right. He had been cruel in his handling of Jane. Jane was almost, if not quite, beautiful. The long lines of her were pure Greek. It was that eager anxiety of hers to please that made her awkward. He had seized on that — exaggerated it — had sharpened the line of her slightly pointed chin, flung her body into an ugly pose.

Why? Why was it impossible for him to be five minutes in the room with Jane without feeling violent irritation against her rising up in him? Say what you would, Jane was a dear but irritating. He was never soothed and at peace with her as he was with Isobel. And yet Jane was so anxious to please, so willing to agree with all he said, but alas! so transparently unable to conceal her real feelings.

He looked round the room. Typically Jane. Some lovely things, pure gems, that piece of

Battersea enamel, for instance, and there next to it, an atrocity of a vase hand painted with roses.

He picked the latter up.

"Would you be very angry, Jane, if I pitched this out of the window?"

"Oh! Alan, you mustn't."

"What do you want with all this trash? You've plenty of taste if you care to use it. Mixing things up!"

"I know, Alan. It isn't that I don't *know*. But people give me things. That vase — Miss Bates brought it back from Margate — and she's so poor, and has to scrape, and it must have cost her quite a lot — for her, you know, and she thought I'd be so pleased. I simply had to put it in a good place."

Everard said nothing. He went on looking around the room. There were one or two etchings on the walls — there were also a number of photographs of babies. Babies, whatever their mothers may think, do not always photograph well. Any of Jane's friends who acquired babies hurried to send photographs of them to her, expecting these tokens to be cherished. Jane had duly cherished them.

"Who's this little horror?" asked Everard, inspecting a pudgy addition with a squint. "I've not seen him before."

"It's a her," said Jane. "Mary Carrington's new baby."

"Poor Mary Carrington," said Everard. "I suppose you'll pretend that you like having that atrocious infant squinting at you all day?"

Jane's chin shot out.

"She's a lovely baby. Mary is a very old friend of mine."

"Loyal Jane," said Everard smiling at her. "So Isobel landed you with Winnie, did she?"

"Well, she did say you wanted to go to Scotland, and I jumped at it. You will let me have Winnie, won't you? I've been wondering if you would let her come to me for ages, but I haven't liked to ask."

"Oh, you can have her — but it's awfully good of you."

"Then that's all right," said Jane happily.

Everard lit a cigarette.

"Isobel show you the new portrait?" he asked rather indistinctly.

"She did."

"What did you think of it?"

Jane's answer came quickly — too quickly:

"It's perfectly splendid. Absolutely splendid."

Alan sprang suddenly to his feet. The hand that held the cigarette shook.

"Damn you, Jane, don't lie to me!"

"But, Alan, I'm sure, it *is* perfectly splendid."

"Haven't you learned by now, Jane, that I know every tone of your voice? You lie to me like a hatter so as not to hurt my feelings, I suppose. Why can't you be honest? Do you think I want you to tell me a thing is splendid when I know as well as you do that it's not? The damned thing's dead — dead. There's no life in it — nothing behind, nothing but surface, damned smooth surface. I've cheated myself all along — yes, even this afternoon. I came along to you to find out. Isobel doesn't know. But you know, you always do know. I knew you'd tell me it was good — you've no moral sense about that sort of thing. But I can tell by the tone of your voice. When I showed you *Romance* you didn't say anything at all — you held your breath and gave a sort of gasp."

"Alan —"

Everard gave her no chance to speak. Jane was producing the effect upon him he knew so well. Strange that so gentle a creature could stir him to such furious anger.

"You think I've lost the power, perhaps," he said angrily, "but I haven't. I can do work every bit as good as *Romance* — better, perhaps. I'll show you, Jane Haworth."

He fairly rushed out of the flat. Walking rapidly, he crossed through the Park and over Albert Bridge. He was still tingling all over with irritation and baffled rage. Jane, indeed! What did *she* know about painting? What was *her* opinion worth? Why should he care? But he did care. He wanted to paint something that would make Jane gasp. Her mouth would open just a little, and her cheeks would flush red. She would look first at the picture and then at him. She wouldn't say anything at all probably.

In the middle of the bridge he saw the picture he was going to paint. It came to him from nowhere at all, out of the blue. He saw it, there in the air, or was it in his head?

A little, dingy curio shop, rather dark and musty looking. Behind the counter a Jew — a small Jew with cunning eyes. In front of him the customer, a big man, sleek, well fed, opulent, bloated, a great jowl on him. Above them, on a shelf, a bust of white marble. The light there, on the boy's marble face, the deathless beauty of old Greece, scornful, unheeding of sale and barter. The Jew, the rich collector, the Greek boy's head. He saw them all.

"*The Connoisseur*, that's what I'll call it," muttered Alan Everard, stepping off the curb and just missing being annihilated by a passing bus. "Yes, *The Connoisseur*: I'll *show* Jane."

When he arrived home, he passed straight into the studio. Isobel found him there, sorting out canvases.

"Alan, don't forget we're dining with the Marches —"

Everard shook his head impatiently.

"Damn the Marches. I'm going to work. I've got hold of something, but I must get it fixed — fixed at once on the canvas before it goes. Ring them up. Tell them I'm dead."

Isobel looked at him thoughtfully for a moment or two, and then went out. She understood the art of living with a genius very thoroughly. She went to the telephone and made some plausible excuse.

She looked round her, yawning a little. Then she sat down at her desk and began to write.

Dear Jane,
Many thanks for your cheque received today. You are good to your godchild. A hundred pounds will do all sorts of things. Children are a terrible expense. You are so fond of Winnie that I felt I was not doing wrong in coming to you for help. Alan, like all geniuses, can only work at what he wants to work at — and unfortunately that doesn't always keep the pot boiling. Hope to see you soon.
Yours,
Isobel

★ ★ ★

When *The Connoisseur* was finished, some months later, Alan invited Jane to come and see it. The thing was not quite as he had conceived it — that was impossible to hope for — but it was near enough. He felt the glow of the creator. He had made this thing and it was good.

Jane did not this time tell him it was splendid. The color crept into her cheeks and her lips parted. She looked at Alan, and he saw in her eyes that which he wished to see. Jane knew.

He walked on air. He had shown Jane!

The picture off his mind, he began to notice his immediate surroundings once more.

Winnie had benefited enormously from her fortnight at the seaside, but it struck him that her clothes were very shabby. He said so to Isobel.

"Alan! You who never notice anything! But I like children to be simply dressed — I hate them all fussed up."

"There's a difference between simplicity and darns and patches."

Isobel said nothing, but she got Winnie a new frock.

Two days later Alan was struggling with income-tax returns. His own passbook lay in front of him. He was hunting through Is-

171

obel's desk for hers when Winnie danced into the room with a disreputable doll.

"Daddy, I've got a riddle. Can you guess it? 'Within a wall as white as milk, within a curtain soft as silk, bathed in a sea of crystal clear, a golden apple doth appear.' Guess what that is?"

"Your mother," said Alan absently. He was still hunting.

"Daddy!" Winnie gave a scream of laughter. "It's an *egg*. Why did you think it was Mummy?"

Alan smiled too.

"I wasn't really listening," he said. "And the words sounded like Mummy, somehow."

A wall as white as milk. A curtain. Crystal. The golden apple. Yes, it did suggest Isobel to him. Curious things, words.

He had found the passbook now. He ordered Winnie peremptorily from the room. Ten minutes later he looked up, startled by a sharp ejaculation.

"Alan!"

"Hullo, Isobel. I didn't hear you come in. Look here, I can't make out these items in your passbook."

"What business had you to touch my passbook?"

He stared at her, astonished. She was angry. He had never seen her angry before.

"I had no idea you would mind."

"I do mind — very much indeed. You have no business to touch my things."

Alan suddenly became angry too.

"I apologize. But since I have touched your things, perhaps you will explain one or two entries that puzzle me. As far as I can see, nearly five hundred pounds has been paid into your account this year which I cannot check. Where does it come from?"

Isobel had recovered her temper. She sank into a chair.

"You needn't be so solemn about it, Alan," she said lightly. "It isn't the wages of sin, or anything like that."

"Where did this money come from?"

"From a woman. A friend of yours. It's not mine at all. It's for Winnie."

"Winnie? Do you mean — this money came from Jane?"

Isobel nodded.

"She's devoted to the child — can't do enough for her."

"Yes, but — surely the money ought to have been invested for Winnie."

"Oh! it isn't that sort of thing at all. It's for current expenses, clothes and all that."

Alan said nothing. He was thinking of Winnie's frocks — all darns and patches.

"Your account's overdrawn, too, Isobel?"

"Is it? That's always happening to me."

"Yes, but that five hundred —"

"My dear Alan. I've spent it on Winnie in the way that seemed best to me. I can assure you Jane is quite satisfied."

Alan was *not* satisfied. Yet such was the power of Isobel's calm that he said nothing more. After all, Isobel was careless in money matters. She hadn't meant to use for herself money given to her for the child. A receipted bill came that day addressed by a mistake to Mr. Everard. It was from a dressmaker in Hanover Square and was for two hundred odd pounds. He gave it to Isobel without a word. She glanced over it, smiled, and said: "Poor boy, I suppose it seems an awful lot to you, but one really *must* be more or less clothed."

The next day he went to see Jane.

Jane was irritating and elusive as usual. He wasn't to bother. Winnie was her godchild. Women understood these things, men didn't. Of course she didn't want Winnie to have five hundred pounds' worth of frocks. Would he please leave it to her and Isobel? They understood each other perfectly.

Alan went away in a state of growing dissatisfaction. He knew perfectly well that he had shirked the one question he really wished to ask. He wanted to say: "Has Isobel ever asked you for money for Winnie?" He didn't say it because he was afraid that Jane might not lie well enough to deceive him.

But he was worried. Jane was poor. He knew she was poor. She mustn't — mustn't denude herself. He made up his mind to speak to Isobel. Isobel was calm and reassuring. Of course she wouldn't let Jane spend more than she could afford.

A month later Jane died.

It was influenza, followed by pneumonia. She made Alan Everard her executor and left all she had to Winnie. But it wasn't very much.

It was Alan's task to go through Jane's papers. She left a record there that was clear to follow — numerous evidences of acts of kindness, begging letters, grateful letters.

And lastly, he found her diary. With it was a scrap of paper: "To be read after my death by Alan Everard. He has often reproached me with not speaking the truth. The truth is all here."

So he came to know at last, finding the one place where Jane had dared to be honest. It was a record, very simple and unforced, of her love for him.

There was very little sentiment about it — no fine language. But there was no blinking of facts.

"I know you are often irritated by me," she had written. "Everything I do or say seems to make you angry sometimes. I do not know why this should be, for I try so hard to please you; but I do believe, all the same, that I mean something real to you. One isn't angry with the people who don't count."

It was not Jane's fault that Alan found other matters. Jane was loyal — but she was also untidy; she filled her drawers too full. She had, shortly before her death, burned carefully all Isobel's letters. The one Alan found was wedged behind a drawer. When he had read it, the meaning of certain caba-listic signs on the counterfoils of Jane's cheque book became clear to him. In this particular letter Isobel had hardly troubled to keep up the pretence of the money being required for Winnie.

Alan sat in front of the desk staring with unseeing eyes out of the window for a long time. Finally he slipped the cheque book into his pocket and left the flat. He walked back to Chelsea, conscious of an anger that grew rapidly stronger.

Isobel was out when he got back, and he was sorry. He had so clearly in his mind what he wanted to say. Instead, he went up to the studio and pulled out the unfinished portrait of Jane. He set it on an easel near the portrait of Isobel in pink satin.

The Lemprière woman had been right: there was life in Jane's portrait. He looked at her, the eager eyes, the beauty that he had tried so unsuccessfully to deny her. That was Jane — the aliveness, more than anything else, was Jane. She was, he thought, the most alive person he had ever met, so much so, that even now he could not think of her as dead.

And he thought of his other pictures — *Color*, *Romance*, Sir Rufus Herschman. They had all, in a way, been pictures of Jane. She had kindled the spark for each one of them — had sent him away fuming and fretting — to *show* her! And now? Jane was dead. Would he ever paint a picture — a real picture — again? He looked again at the eager face on the canvas. Perhaps. Jane wasn't very far away.

A sound made him wheel round. Isobel had come into the studio. She was dressed for dinner in a straight white gown that showed up the pure gold of her hair.

She stopped dead and checked the words on her lips. Eyeing him warily, she went over to the divan and sat down. She had every appearance of calm.

Alan took the cheque book from his pocket.

"I've been going through Jane's papers."

"Yes?"

He tried to imitate her calm, to keep his voice from shaking.

"For the last four years she's been supplying you with money."

"Yes. For Winnie."

"No, not for Winnie," shouted Everard. "You pretended, both of you, that it was for Winnie, but you both knew that that wasn't so. Do you realize that Jane has been selling her securities, living from hand to mouth, to supply you with clothes — clothes that you didn't really need?"

Isobel never took her eyes from his face. She settled her body more comfortably on the cushions as a white Persian cat might do.

"I can't help it if Jane denuded herself more than she should have done," she said. "I supposed she could afford the money. She was always crazy about you — I could see that, of course. Some wives would have kicked up a fuss about the way you were always rushing off to see her, and spending hours there. I didn't."

"No," said Alan, very white in the face. "You made her pay instead."

"You are saying very offensive things, Alan. Be careful."

"Aren't they true? Why did you find it so easy to get money out of Jane?"

"Not for love of me, certainly. It must have been for love of you."

"That's just what it was," said Alan simply. "She paid for my freedom — freedom to work in my own way. So long as you had a sufficiency of money, you'd leave me alone — not badger me to paint a crowd of awful women."

Isobel said nothing.

"Well?" cried Alan angrily.

Her quiescence infuriated him.

Isobel was looking at the floor. Presently she raised her head and said quietly:

"Come here, Alan."

She touched the divan at her side. Uneasily, unwillingly, he came and sat there, not looking at her. But he knew that he was afraid.

"Alan," said Isobel presently.

"Well?"

He was irritable, nervous.

"All that you say may be true. It doesn't matter. I'm like that. I want things — clothes, money, *you*. *Jane's dead*, Alan."

"What do you mean?"

"Jane's dead. You belong to me altogether now. You never did before — not quite."

He looked at her — saw the light in her eyes, acquisitive, possessive — was revolted yet fascinated.

"Now you shall be all mine."

He understood Isobel then as he had never understood her before.

"You want me as a slave? I'm to paint what you tell me to paint, live as you tell me to live, be dragged at your chariot wheels."

"Put it like that if you please. What are words?"

He felt her arms round his neck, white, smooth, firm as a wall. Words danced through his brain. "A wall as white as milk." Already he was inside the wall. Could he still escape? Did he want to escape?

He heard her voice close against his ear — poppy and mandragora.

"What else is there to live for? Isn't this enough? Love — happiness — success — love —"

The wall was growing up all around him now — "the curtain soft as silk," the curtain wrapping him round, stifling him a little, but so soft, so sweet! Now they were drifting together, at peace, out on the crystal sea. The wall was very high now, shutting out all those other things — those dangerous, disturbing things that hurt — that always hurt. Out on the sea of crystal, the golden apple between their hands.

The light faded from Jane's picture.

VIII

The Mystery of
the Spanish Chest

Punctual to the moment, as always, Hercule
Poirot entered the small room where Miss
Lemon, his efficient secretary, awaited her
instructions for the day.

At first sight Miss Lemon seemed to be
composed entirely of angles — thus satisfy-
ing Poirot's demand for symmetry.

Not that where women were concerned
Hercule Poirot carried his passion for geo-
metrical precision so far. He was, on the
contrary, old-fashioned. He had a continen-
tal prejudice for curves — it might be said
for voluptuous curves. He liked women to
be women. He liked them lush, highly colored, exotic. There had been a certain Rus-
sian countess — but that was long ago now.
A folly of earlier days.

But Miss Lemon he had never considered
as a woman. She was a human machine —
an instrument of precision. Her efficiency
was terrific. She was forty-eight years of age,

and was fortunate enough to have no imagination whatever.

"Good morning, Miss Lemon."

"Good morning, M. Poirot."

Poirot sat down and Miss Lemon placed before him the morning's mail, neatly arranged in categories. She resumed her seat and sat with pad and pencil at the ready.

But there was to be this morning a slight change in routine. Poirot had brought in with him the morning newspaper, and his eyes were scanning it with interest. The headlines were big and bold. "SPANISH CHEST MYSTERY. LATEST DEVELOPMENTS."

"You have read the morning papers, I presume, Miss Lemon?"

"Yes, M. Poirot. The news from Geneva is not very good."

Poirot waved away the news from Geneva in a comprehensive sweep of the arm.

"A Spanish chest," he mused. "Can you tell me, Miss Lemon, what exactly is a Spanish chest?"

"I suppose, M. Poirot, that it is a chest that came originally from Spain."

"One might reasonably suppose so. You have then, no expert knowledge?"

"They are usually of the Elizabethan period, I believe. Large, and with a good deal of brass decoration on them. They look very nice when well kept and polished. My sister bought one at a sale. She keeps household linen in it. It looks very nice."

"I am sure that in the house of any sister of yours, all the furniture would be well kept," said Poirot, bowing gracefully.

Miss Lemon replied sadly that servants did not seem to know what elbow grease *was* nowadays. Poirot looked a little puzzled, but decided not to inquire into the inward meaning of the mysterious phrase "elbow grease."

He looked down again at the newspaper, conning over the names: Major Rich, Mr. and Mrs. Clayton, Commander McLaren, Mr. and Mrs. Spence. Names, nothing but names to him; yet all possessed of human personalities, hating, loving, fearing. A drama, this, in which he, Hercule Poirot, had no part. And he would have liked to have a part in it! Six people at an evening party, in a room with a big Spanish chest against the wall, six people, five of them talking, eating a buffet supper, putting records on the gramophone, dancing, and the sixth *dead, in the Spanish chest. . . .*

Ah, thought Poirot. How my dear friend Hastings would have enjoyed this! What romantic flights of imagination he would have had. What ineptitudes he would have uttered! Ah, *ce cher Hastings,* at this moment, today, I miss him. . . . Instead —

He sighed and looked at Miss Lemon. Miss Lemon, intelligently perceiving that Poirot was in no mood to dictate letters, had uncovered her typewriter and was awaiting her moment to get on with certain arrears of work. Nothing could have interested her less than sinister Spanish chests containing dead bodies.

Poirot sighed and looked down at a photographed face. Reproductions in newsprint were never very good, and this was decidedly smudgy — but what a face! *Mrs. Clayton, the wife of the murdered man.* . . .

On an impulse, he thrust the paper at Miss Lemon.

"Look," he demanded. "Look at that face."

Miss Lemon looked at it obediently, without emotion.

"What do you think of her, Miss Lemon? That is Mrs. Clayton."

Miss Lemon took the paper, glanced casually at the picture, and remarked:

"She's a little like the wife of our bank manager when we lived at Croydon Heath."

"Interesting," said Poirot. "Recount to me, if you will be so kind, the history of your bank manager's wife."

"Well, it's not really a very pleasant story, M. Poirot."

"It was in my mind that it might not be. Continue."

"There was a good deal of talk — about Mrs. Adams and a young artist. Then Mr. Adams shot himself. But Mrs. Adams wouldn't marry the other man and he took some kind of poison — but they pulled him through all right; and finally Mrs. Adams married a young solicitor. I believe there was more trouble after that, only of course we'd left Croydon Heath by then so I didn't hear very much more about it."

Hercule Poirot nodded gravely.

"She was beautiful?"

"Well — not really what you'd call beautiful — But there seemed to be something about her —"

"Exactly. What is that something that they possess — the sirens of this world! The Helens of Troy, the Cleopatras — ?"

Miss Lemon inserted a piece of paper vigorously into her typewriter.

"Really, M. Poirot, I've never thought about it. It seems all very silly to me. If people would just go on with their jobs and didn't think about such things it would be much better."

Having thus disposed of human frailty and

185

passion, Miss Lemon let her fingers hover over the keys of the typewriter, waiting impatiently to be allowed to begin her work.

"That is your view," said Poirot. "And at this moment it is your desire that *you* should be allowed to get on with *your* job. But your job, Miss Lemon, is not only to take down my letters, to file my papers, to deal with my telephone calls, to typewrite my letters — All these things you do admirably. But me, I deal not only with documents but with human beings. And there, too, I need assistance."

"Certainly, M. Poirot," said Miss Lemon patiently. "What is it you want me to do?"

"This case interests me. I should be glad if you would make a study of this morning's report of it in all the papers and also of any additional reports in the evening papers — Make me a précis of the facts."

"Very good, M. Poirot."

Poirot withdrew to his sitting room, a rueful smile on his face.

"It is indeed the irony," he said to himself, "that after my dear friend Hastings I should have Miss Lemon. What greater contrast can one imagine? *Ce cher Hastings* — how he would have enjoyed himself. How he would have walked up and down talking about it, putting the most romantic construction on

186

every incident, believing as gospel truth every word the papers have printed about it. And my poor Miss Lemon, what I have asked her to do, she will not enjoy at all!"

Miss Lemon came to him in due course with a typewritten sheet.

"I've got the information you wanted, M. Poirot. I'm afraid though, it can't be regarded as reliable. The papers vary a good deal in their accounts. I shouldn't like to guarantee that the facts as stated are more than sixty per cent accurate."

"That is probably a conservative estimate," murmured Poirot. "Thank you, Miss Lemon, for the trouble you have taken."

The facts were sensational but clear enough. Major Charles Rich, a well-to-do-bachelor, had given an evening party to a few of his friends, at his apartment. These friends consisted of Mr. and Mrs. Clayton, Mr. and Mrs. Spence, and a Commander McLaren. Commander McLaren was a very old friend of both Rich and the Claytons, Mr. and Mrs. Spence, a younger couple, were fairly recent acquaintances. Arnold Clayton was in the Treasury. Jeremy Spence was a junior civil servant. Major Rich was forty-eight, Arnold Clayton was fifty-five, Commander McLaren was forty-six, Jeremy Spence was thirty-seven. Mrs. Clayton was said to be "some years younger than her husband." One person was unable to attend the party. At the last moment, Mr. Clayton was called away to Scotland on urgent business, and was supposed to have left King's Cross by the 8:15 train.

The party proceeded as such parties do. Everyone appeared to be enjoying themselves. It was neither a wild party nor a drunken one. It broke up about 11:45. The four guests left together and shared a taxi. Commander McLaren was dropped first at his club and then the Spences dropped Margharita Clayton at Cardigan Gardens just off Sloane Street and went on themselves to their house in Chelsea.

The gruesome discovery was made on the following morning by Major Rich's manservant, William Burgess. The latter did not live in. He arrived early so as to clear up the sitting room before calling Major Rich with his early morning tea. It was whilst clearing up that Burgess was startled to find a big stain discoloring the light-colored rug on which stood the Spanish chest. It seemed to have seeped through from the chest, and the valet immediately lifted up the lid of the chest and looked inside. He was horrified to find there the body of Mr. Clayton, stabbed through the neck.

Obeying his first impulse, Burgess rushed out into the street and fetched the nearest policeman.

Such were the bald facts of the case. But there were further details. The police had immediately broken the news to Mrs. Clayton, who had been "completely prostrated." She had seen her husband for the last time at a little after six o'clock on the evening before. He had come home much annoyed, having been summoned to Scotland on urgent business in connection with some property that he owned. He had urged his wife to go to the party without him. Mr. Clayton had then called in at his and Commander McLaren's club, had had a drink with his friend, and had explained the position. He had then said, looking at his watch, that he had just time on his way to King's Cross, to call in on Major Rich and explain. He had already tried to telephone him, but the line had seemed to be out of order.

According to William Burgess, Mr. Clayton arrived at the flat at about 7:55. Major Rich was out but was due to return any moment, so Burgess suggested that Mr. Clayton should come in and wait. Clayton said he had no time but would come in and write a note. He explained that he was on his way to catch a train at King's Cross. The valet showed him into the sitting room and himself returned to the kitchen, where he was engaged in the preparation of canapés for the party. The valet did not hear his master return, but about ten minutes later, Major Rich looked into the kitchen and told Burgess to hurry out and get some Turkish cigarettes, which were Mrs. Spence's favorite smoking. The valet did so and brought them to his master in the sitting room. Mr. Clayton was not there, but the valet naturally thought he had already left to catch his train.

Major Rich's story was short and simple. Mr. Clayton was not in the flat when he himself came in and he had no idea that he had been there. No note had been left for him and the first he heard of Mr. Clayton's journey to Scotland was when Mrs. Clayton and the others arrived.

There were two additional items in the evening papers. Mrs. Clayton who was "prostrated with shock" had left her flat in Cardigan Gardens and was believed to be staying with friends.

The second item was in the stop press. Major Charles Rich had been charged with the murder of Arnold Clayton and had been taken into custody.

"So that is that," said Poirot, looking up at Miss Lemon. "The arrest of Major Rich was to be expected. But what a remarkable case. What a *very* remarkable case! Do you not think so?"

"I suppose such things do happen, M. Poirot," said Miss Lemon without interest.

"Oh certainly! They happen every day. Or nearly every day. But usually they are quite understandable — though distressing."

"It is certainly a very unpleasant business."

"To be stabbed to death and stowed away in a Spanish chest is certainly unpleasant for the victim — supremely so. But when I say this is a remarkable case, I refer to the remarkable behavior of Major Rich."

Miss Lemon said with faint distaste:

"There seems to be a suggestion that Major Rich and Mrs. Clayton were very close friends. . . . It was a suggestion and not a proved fact, so I did not include it."

"That was very correct of you. But it is an inference that leaps to the eye. Is that all you have to say?"

Miss Lemon looked blank. Poirot sighed, and missed the rich colorful imagination of his friend Hastings. Discussing a case with Miss Lemon was uphill work.

"Consider for a moment this Major Rich. He is in love with Mrs. Clayton — granted. . . . He wants to dispose of her husband —

191

that, too, we grant, though if Mrs. Clayton is in love with him, and they are having the affair together, where is the urgency? It is, perhaps, that Mr. Clayton will not give his wife the divorce? But it is not of all this that I talk. Major Rich, he is a retired soldier, and it is said sometimes that soldiers are not brainy. But, *tout de même,* this Major Rich, is he, can he be, a complete imbecile?"

Miss Lemon did not reply. She took this to be a purely rhetorical question.

"Well," demanded Poirot. "What do *you* think about it all?"

"What do *I* think?" Miss Lemon was startled.

"*Mais oui* — you!"

Miss Lemon adjusted her mind to the strain put upon it. She was not given to mental speculation of any kind unless asked for it. In such leisure moments as she had, her mind was filled with the details of a superlatively perfect filing system. It was her only mental recreation.

"Well —" she began, and paused.

"Tell me just what happened — what you think happened, on that evening. Mr. Clayton is in the sitting room writing a note, Major Rich comes back — what then?"

"He finds Mr. Clayton there. They — I suppose they have a quarrel. Major Rich

192

stabs him. Then, when he sees what he has done, he — he puts the body in the chest. After all, the guests, I suppose, might be arriving any minute."

"Yes, yes. The guests arrive! The body is in the chest. The evening passes. The guests depart. And then —"

"Well, then, I suppose Major Rich goes to bed and — Oh!"

"Ah," said Poirot. "You see it now. You have murdered a man. You have concealed his body in a chest. And then — you go peacefully to bed, quite unperturbed by the fact that your valet will discover the crime in the morning."

"I suppose it's possible that the valet might never have looked inside the chest?"

"With an enormous pool of blood on the carpet underneath it?"

"Perhaps Major Rich didn't realize that the blood was there."

"Was it not somewhat careless of him not to look and see?"

"I dare say he was upset," said Miss Lemon.

Poirot threw up his hands in despair.

Miss Lemon seized the opportunity to hurry from the room.

The mystery of the Spanish chest was,

strictly speaking, no business of Poirot's. He was engaged at the moment in a delicate mission for one of the large oil companies where one of the high ups was possibly involved in some questionable transaction. It was hush-hush, important, and exceedingly lucrative. It was sufficiently involved to command Poirot's attention, and had the great advantage that it required very little physical activity. It was sophisticated and bloodless. Crime at the highest levels.

The mystery of the Spanish chest was dramatic and emotional, two qualities which Poirot had often declared to Hastings could be much overrated — and indeed frequently were so by the latter. He had been severe with *ce cher Hastings* on this point, and now here he was, behaving much as his friend might have done, obsessed with beautiful women, crimes of passion, jealousy, hatred, and all the other romantic causes of murder! He wanted to *know* about it all. He wanted to know what Major Rich was like, and what his manservant, Burgess, was like, and what Margharita Clayton was like (though that, he thought, he knew) and what the late Arnold Clayton had been like (since he held that the character of the victim was of the first importance in a murder case), and even what Commander McLaren, the faithful friend, and Mr. and Mrs. Spence, the recently acquired acquaintances, were like.

And he did not see exactly how he was going to gratify his curiosity!

He reflected on the matter later in the day.

Why did the whole business intrigue him so much? He decided, after reflection, that it was because — as the facts were related — the whole thing was more or less impossible! Yes, there was a Euclidean flavor.

Starting from what one could accept, there had been a quarrel between two men. Cause, presumably, a woman. One man killed the other in the heat of rage. Yes, that happened — though it would be more acceptable if the husband had killed the lover. Still — the lover had killed the husband, stabbed him with a dagger (?) — somehow a rather unlikely weapon. Perhaps Major Rich had had an Italian mother? Somewhere — surely — there should be something to explain the choice of a dagger as a weapon. Anyway, one must accept the dagger (some papers called it a stiletto!). It was to hand and was used. The body was concealed in the chest. That was common sense and inevitable. The crime had not been premeditated, and as the valet was returning at any moment, and four guests would be arriving before very long, it seemed the only course indicated.

The party is held, the guests depart, the manservant is already gone — and — Major Rich goes to bed!

To understand how that could happen, one must see Major Rich and find out what kind of a man acts in that way.

Could it be that, overcome with horror at what he had done and the long strain of an evening trying to appear his normal self, he had taken a sleeping pill of some kind or a tranquilizer which had put him into a heavy slumber which lasted long beyond his usual hour of waking? Possible. Or was it a case, rewarding to a psychologist, where Major Rich's feeling of subconscious guilt made him *want* the crime to be discovered? To make up one's mind on that point one would have to see Major Rich. It all came back to —

The telephone rang. Poirot let it ring for some moments, until he realized that Miss Lemon after bringing him his letters to sign, had gone home some time ago, and that George had probably gone out.

He picked up the receiver.

"M. Poirot?"

"Speaking!"

"Oh how splendid." Poirot blinked slightly at the fervor of the charming female voice. "It's Abbie Chatterton."

"Ah, Lady Chatterton. How can I serve you?"

"By coming over as quickly as you can right away to a simply frightful cocktail party I am giving. Not just for the cocktail party — it's for something quite different really. I *need* you. It's absolutely *vital.* Please, *please, please* don't let me down! *Don't* say you can't manage it."

Poirot had not been going to say anything of the kind. Lord Chatterton, apart from being a peer of the realm and occasionally making a very dull speech in the House of Lords, was nobody in particular. But Lady Chatterton was one of the brightest jewels in what Poirot called *le haut monde.* Everything she did or said was news. She had brains, beauty, originality, and enough vitality to activate a rocket to the moon.

She said again:

"I *need* you. Just give that wonderful moustache of yours a lovely twirl, and *come!*"

It was not quite so quick as that. Poirot had first to make a meticulous toilet. The twirl to the moustaches was added and he then set off.

The door of Lady Chatterton's delightful house in Cheriton Street was ajar and a noise as of animals mutinying at the zoo sounded from within. Lady Chatterton, who was

197

holding two ambassadors, an international rugger player, and an American evangelist in play, neatly jettisoned them with the rapidity of sleight of hand and was at Poirot's side.

"M. Poirot, how wonderful to see you! No, don't have that nasty Martini. I've got something special for you — a kind of *sirop* that the sheikhs drink in Morocco. It's in my own little room upstairs."

She led the way upstairs and Poirot followed her. She paused to say over her shoulder:

"I didn't put these people off, because it's absolutely essential that no one should know there's anything special going on here, and I've promised the servants enormous bonuses if not a word leaks out. After all, one doesn't want one's house besieged by reporters. And, poor darling, she's been through so much already."

Lady Chatterton did not stop at the first-floor landing; instead she swept on up to the floor above.

Gasping for breath and somewhat bewildered, Hercule Poirot followed.

Lady Chatterton paused, gave a rapid glance downwards over the banisters, and then flung open a door, exclaiming as she did so:

"I've got him, Margharita! I've got him! Here he is!"

She stood aside in triumph to let Poirot enter, then performed a rapid introduction.

"This is Margharita Clayton. She's a very, very dear friend of mine. You'll help her, won't you? Margharita, this is that wonderful Hercule Poirot. He'll do just everything you want — you will, won't you, dear M. Poirot?"

And without waiting for the answer which she obviously took for granted (Lady Chatterton had not been a spoiled beauty all her life for nothing), she dashed out of the door and down the stairs, calling back rather indiscreetly, "I've got to go back to all these awful people. . . ."

The woman who had been sitting in a chair by the window rose and came towards him. He would have recognized her even if Lady Chatterton had not mentioned her name. Here was that wide, that very wide brow, the dark hair that sprang away from it like wings, the grey eyes set far apart. She wore a close-fitting high-necked gown of dull black that showed up the beauty of her body and the magnolia-whiteness of her skin. It was an unusual face rather than a beautiful one — one of those oddly proportioned faces that one sometimes sees in an Italian primitive. There was about her a kind of medieval simplicity — a strange innocence that could be, Poirot thought, more devastating than any voluptuous sophistication. When she spoke it was with a kind of childlike candor.

"Abbie says you will help me. . . ."

She looked at him gravely and inquiringly.

For a moment he stood quite still, scrutinizing her closely. There was nothing ill-bred in his manner of doing it. It was more the kind but searching look that a famous consultant gives a new patient.

"Are you sure, madame," he said at last, "that I *can* help you?"

A little flush rose to her cheeks.

"I don't know what you mean."

"What is it, madame, that you want me to do?"

"Oh," she seemed surprised. "I thought — you knew who I was?"

"I know who you are. Your husband was killed — stabbed, and a Major Rich has been arrested and charged with his murder."

The flush heightened.

"Major Rich did *not* kill my husband."

Quick as a flash Poirot said:

"Why not?"

She stared, puzzled. "I — I beg your pardon?"

"I have confused you — because I have not asked the question that everybody asks — the police — the lawyers. . . . 'Why should

Major Rich kill Arnold Clayton?' But I ask the opposite. I ask you, madame, why you are sure that Major Rich did *not* kill him?"

"Because" — she paused a moment — "because I know Major Rich so well."

"You know Major Rich so well," repeated Poirot tonelessly.

He paused and then said sharply:

"How well?"

Whether she understood his meaning, he could not guess. He thought to himself: Here is either a woman of great simplicity or of great subtlety. . . . Many people, he thought, must have wondered that about Margharita Clayton. . . .

"How well?" She was looking at him doubtfully. "Five years — no, nearly six."

"That was not precisely what I meant. . . . You must understand, madame, that I shall have to ask you the impertinent questions. Perhaps you will speak the truth, perhaps you will lie. It is very necessary for a woman to lie sometimes. Women must defend themselves, and the lie, it can be a good weapon. But there are three people, madame, to whom a woman should speak the truth. To her Father confessor, to her hairdresser, and to her private detective — if she trusts him. Do you trust me, madame?"

Margharita Clayton drew a deep breath.

"Yes," she said. "I do." And added: "I must."

"Very well, then. What is it you want me to do — find out who killed your husband?"

"I suppose so — yes."

"But it is not essential? You want me, then, to clear Major Rich from suspicion?"

She nodded quickly — gratefully.

"That — and that only?"

It was, he saw, an unnecessary question. Margharita Clayton was a woman who saw only one thing at a time.

"And now," he said, "for the impertinence. You and Major Rich, you are lovers, yes?"

"Do you mean, were we having an affair together? No."

"But he was in love with you?"

"Yes."

"And you — were in love with him?"

"I think so."

"You do not seem quite sure?"

"I *am* sure — now."

"Ah! You did not, then, love your husband?"

"No."

"You reply with an admirable simplicity. Most women would wish to explain at great length just exactly what their feelings were. How long had you been married?"

202

"Eleven years."

"Can you tell me a little about your husband — what kind of a man he was?"

She frowned.

"It's difficult. I don't really know what kind of a man Arnold was. He was very quiet — very reserved. One didn't know what he was thinking. He was clever, of course — everyone said he was brilliant — in his work, I mean. . . . He didn't — how can I put it — he never explained himself at all. . . ."

"Was he in love with you?"

"Oh, yes. He must have been. Or he wouldn't have minded so much —" she came to a sudden stop.

"About other men? That is what you were going to say? He was jealous?"

Again she said:

"He must have been." And then, as though feeling that the phrase needed explanation, she went on. "Sometimes, for days, he wouldn't speak. . . ."

Poirot nodded thoughtfully.

"This violence — that has come into your life. Is it the first that you have known?"

"Violence?" She frowned, then flushed. "Is it — do you mean — that poor boy who shot himself?"

"Yes," said Poirot. "I expect that is what I mean."

"I'd no idea he felt like that . . . I was sorry for him — he seemed so shy — so lonely. He must have been very neurotic, I think. And there were two Italians — a duel — It was ridiculous! Anyway, nobody was killed, thank goodness. . . . And honestly, I didn't care about *either* of them! I never even pretended to care."

"No. You were just — there! And where you are — things happen! I have seen that before in my life. It is *because* you do not care that men are driven mad. But for Major Rich you do care. So — we must do what we can. . . ."

He was silent for a moment or two.

She sat there gravely, watching him.

"We turn from personalities, which are often the really important things, to plain facts. I know only what has been in the papers. On the facts as given there, only two persons had the opportunity of killing your husband, only two persons *could* have killed him — Major Rich and Major Rich's man-servant."

She said, stubbornly:

"I *know* Charles didn't kill him."

"So, then, it must have been the valet. You agree?"

She said doubtfully:

"I see what you mean. . . ."

204

"But you are dubious about it?"

"It just seems — fantastic!"

"Yet the *possibility* is there. Your husband undoubtedly came to the flat, since his body was found there. If the valet's story is true, Major Rich killed him. But if the valet's story is false? Then the valet killed him and hid the body in the chest before his master returned. An excellent way of disposing of the body from his point of view. He has only got to 'notice the bloodstain' the next morning and 'discover' it. Suspicion will immediately fall on Rich."

"But why should he want to kill Arnold?"

"Ah why? The motive cannot be an obvious one — or the police would have investigated it. It is possible that your husband knew something to the valet's discredit, and was about to acquaint Major Rich with the facts. Did your husband ever say anything to you about this man Burgess?"

She shook her head.

"Do you think he would have done so — if that had indeed been the case?"

She frowned.

"It's difficult to say. Possibly not. Arnold never talked much about people. I told you he was reserved. He wasn't — he was never — a *chatty* man."

"He was a man who kept his own counsel.

. . . Yes, now what is your opinion of Burgess?"

"He's not the kind of man you notice very much. A fairly good servant. Adequate but not polished."

"What age?"

"About thirty-seven or -eight, I should think. He'd been an orderly in the army during the war, but he wasn't a regular soldier."

"How long had he been with Major Rich?"

"Not very long. About a year and a half, I think."

"You never noticed anything odd about his manner towards your husband?"

"We weren't there so very often. No, I noticed nothing at all."

"Tell me now about the events of that evening. What time were you invited?"

"Eight-fifteen or half past."

"And just what kind of a party was it to be?"

"Well, there would be drinks, and a kind of buffet supper — usually a very good one. Foie gras and hot toast. Smoked salmon. Sometimes there was a hot rice dish — Charles had a special recipe he'd got in the Near East — but that was more for winter. Then we used to have music — Charles had got a very good stereophonic gramophone. Both my husband and Jock McLaren were very fond of classical records. And we had dance music — the Spences were very keen dancers. It was that sort of thing — a quiet informal evening. Charles was a very good host."

"And this particular evening — it was like other evenings there? You noticed nothing unusual — nothing out of place?"

"Out of place?" she frowned for a moment. "When you said that I — no, it's gone. There was something. . . ." She shook her head again. "No. To answer your question, there was nothing unusual at all about that evening. We enjoyed ourselves. Everybody seemed relaxed and happy." She shivered. "And to think that all the time —"

Poirot held up a quick hand.

"Do not think. This business that took your husband to Scotland, how much do you know about that?"

"Not very much. There was some dispute over the restrictions on selling a piece of land which belonged to my husband. The sale had apparently gone through and then some sudden snag turned up."

"What did your husband tell you exactly?"

"He came in with a telegram in his hand. As far as I remember, he said, 'This is most annoying. I shall have to take the night mail to Edinburgh and see Johnston first thing tomorrow morning. . . . Too bad when one thought the thing was going through smoothly at last.' then he said, 'Shall I ring up Jock and get him to call for you?' and I said, 'Nonsense, I'll just take a taxi,' and he said that Jock or the Spences would see me home. I said did he want anything packed and he said he'd just throw a few things into a bag, and have a quick snack at the club, before catching the train. Then he went off and — and that's the last time I saw him."

Her voice broke a little on the last words.

Poirot looked at her very hard.

"Did he show you the telegram?"

"No."

"A pity."

"Why do you say that?"

He did not answer that question. Instead he said briskly:

"Now to business. Who are the solicitors acting for Major Rich?"

She told him and he made a note of the address.

"Will you write a few words to them and give it to me? I shall want to make arrangements to see Major Rich."

"He — it's been remanded for a week."

"Naturally. That is the procedure. Will you also write a note to Commander

McLaren and to your friends the Spences? I shall want to see all of them, and it is essential that they do not at once show me the door."

When she rose from the writing desk, he said:

"One thing more. I shall register my own impressions, but I also want yours — of Commander McLaren and of Mr. and Mrs. Spence."

"Jock is one of our oldest friends. I've known him ever since I was a child. He appears to be quite a dour person, but he's really a dear — always the same — always to be relied upon. He's not gay and amusing but he's a tower of strength — both Arnold and I relied on his judgement a lot."

"And he, also, is doubtless in love with you?" Poirot's eyes twinkled slightly.

"Oh yes," said Margharita happily. "He's always been in love with me — but by now it's become a kind of habit."

"And the Spences?"

"They're amusing — and very good company. Linda Spence is really rather a clever girl. Arnold enjoyed talking with her. She's attractive, too."

"You are friends?"

"She and I? In a way. I don't know that I *really* like her. She's too malicious."

"And her husband?"

"Oh, Jeremy is delightful. Very musical. Knows a good deal about pictures, too. He and I go to picture shows a good deal together. . . ."

"Ah, well, I shall see for myself." He took her hand in his. "I hope, madame, you will not regret asking for my help."

"Why should I regret it?" Her eyes opened wide.

"One never knows," said Poirot cryptically.

"And I — I do not know," he said to himself, as he went down the stairs. The cocktail party was still in full spate, but he avoided being captured and reached the street.

"No," he repeated. "I do not know."

It was of Margharita Clayton he was thinking.

That apparently childlike candor, that frank innocence — Was it just that? Or did it mask something else? There had been women like that in medieval days — women on whom history had not been able to agree. He thought of Mary Stuart, the Scottish Queen. Had she known, that night in Kirk o'Fields, of the deed that was to be done? Or was she completely innocent? Had the conspirators told her nothing? Was she one of those childlike simple women who can say to themselves "I do not know" and believe it? He felt the spell of Margharita Clayton. But he was not entirely sure about her. . . .

Such women could be, though innocent themselves, the cause of crimes.

Such women could be, in intent and design, criminals themselves, though not in action.

Theirs was never the hand that held the knife —

As to Margharita Clayton — no — he did not know!

Hercule Poirot did not find Major Rich's solicitors very helpful. He had not expected to do so.

They managed to indicate, though without saying so, that it would be in their client's best interest if Mrs. Clayton showed no sign of activity on his behalf.

His visit to them was in the interests of "correctness." He had enough pull with the Home Office and the CID to arrange his interview with the prisoner.

Inspector Miller, who was in charge of the Clayton case, was not one of Poirot's favorites. He was not, however, hostile on this occasion, merely contemptuous.

"Can't waste much time over the old dodderer," he had said to his assisting sergeant before Poirot was shown in. "Still, I'll have to be polite."

"You'll really have to pull some rabbits out of a hat if you're going to do anything with this one, M. Poirot," he remarked cheerfully. "Nobody else but Rich *could* have killed the bloke."

"Except the valet."

"Oh, I'll give you the valet! As a possibility, that is. But you won't find anything there. No motives whatever."

"You cannot be entirely sure of that. Motives are very curious things."

"Well, he wasn't acquainted with Clayton in any way. He's got a perfectly innocuous past. And he seems to be perfectly right in his head. I don't know what more you want?"

"I want to find out that Rich did not commit the crime."

"To please the lady, eh?" Inspector Miller grinned wickedly. "She's been getting at you, I suppose. Quite something, isn't she? *Cherchez la femme* with a vengeance. If she'd had the opportunity, you know, she might have done it herself."

"That, *no!*"

"You'd be surprised. I once knew a woman like that. Put a couple of husbands out of the way without a blink of her innocent blue eyes. Broken-hearted each time, too. The jury would have acquitted her if they'd had half a chance — which they hadn't, the evidence being practically cast iron."

"Well, my friend, let us not argue. What I make so bold as to ask is a few reliable details on the facts. What a newspaper prints is news — but not always truth!"

"They have to enjoy themselves. What do you want?"

"Time of death as near as can be."

"Which can't be very near because the body wasn't examined until the following morning. Death is estimated to have taken place from thirteen to ten hours previously. That is, between seven and ten o'clock the night before. . . . He was stabbed through the jugular vein — Death must have been a matter of moments."

"And the weapon?"

"A kind of Italian stiletto — quite small — razor sharp. Nobody has ever seen it before, or knows where it comes from. But we shall know — in the end. . . . It's a matter of time and patience."

"It could not have been picked up in the course of a quarrel."

"No. The valet says no such thing was in the flat."

"What interests me is the telegram," said Poirot. "The telegram that called Arnold Clayton away to Scotland. . . . Was that summons genuine?"

"No. There was no hitch or trouble up there. The land transfer, or whatever it was, was proceeding normally."

"Then who sent that telegram — I am presuming there *was* a telegram?"

"There must have been. . . . Not that we'd necessarily believe Mrs. Clayton. But Clayton told the valet he was called by wire to Scotland. And he also told Commander McLaren."

"What time did he see Commander McLaren?"

"They had a snack together at their club — Combined Services — that was at about a quarter past seven. Then Clayton took a taxi to Rich's flat, arriving there just before eight o'clock. After that —" Miller spread his hands out.

"Anybody notice anything at all odd about Rich's manner that evening?"

"Oh well, you know what people are. Once a thing has happened, people think they noticed a lot of things I bet they never saw at all. Mrs. Spence, now, she says he was *distrait* all the evening. Didn't always answer to the point. As though he had 'something on his mind.' I bet he had, too, if he had a body in the chest! Wondering how the hell to get rid of it!"

"Why didn't he get rid of it?"

"Beats me. Lost his nerve, perhaps. But it was madness to leave it until the next day. He had the best chance he'd ever have that night. There's no night porter on. He could have got his car round, packed the body in the boot — it's a big boot — driven out in the country and parked it somewhere. He might have been seen getting the body into the car, but the flats are in a side street and there's a courtyard you drive a car through. At, say, three in the morning, he had a reasonable chance. And what does he do? Goes to bed, sleeps late the next morning and wakes up to find the police in the flat!"

"He went to bed and slept well as an innocent man might do."

"Have it that way if you like. But do you really believe that yourself?"

"I shall have to leave that question until I have seen the man myself."

"Think you know an innocent man when you see one? It's not so easy as that."

"I know it is not easy — and I should not attempt to say I could do it. What I want to make up my mind about is whether the man is as stupid as he seems to be."

Poirot had no intention of seeing Charles Rich until he had seen everyone else.

He started with Commander McLaren.

McLaren was a tall, swarthy, uncommunicative man. He had a rugged but pleasant face. He was a shy man and not easy to talk to. But Poirot persevered.

Fingering Margharita's note, McLaren said almost reluctantly:

"Well, if Margharita wants me to tell you all I can, of course I'll do so. Don't know what there is to tell, though. You've heard it all already. But whatever Margharita wants — I've always done what she wanted — ever since she was sixteen. She's got a way with her, you know."

"I know," said Poirot. He went on. "First I should like you to answer a question quite frankly. Do you think Major Rich is guilty?"

"Yes, I do. I wouldn't say so to Margharita if she wants to think he's innocent, but I simply can't see it any other way. Hang it all, the fellow's *got* to be guilty."

"Was there bad feeling between him and Mr. Clayton?"

"Not in the least. Arnold and Charles were the best of friends. That's what makes the whole thing so extraordinary."

"Perhaps Major Rich's friendship with

216

Mrs. Clayton —"

He was interrupted.

"Faugh! All that stuff. All the papers slyly hinting at it. . . . Damned innuendoes! Mrs. Clayton and Rich were good friends and that's all! Margharita's got lots of friends. *I'm* her friend. Been one for years. And nothing the whole world mightn't know about it. Same with Charles and Margharita."

"You do not then consider that they were having an affair together?"

"Certainly *NOT!*" McLaren was wrathful. "Don't go listening to that hellcat Spence woman. She'd say anything."

"But perhaps Mr. Clayton suspected there *might* be something between his wife and Major Rich."

"You can take it from me he did nothing of the sort! I'd have known if so. Arnold and I were very close."

"What sort of man was he? You, if anyone, should know."

"Well, Arnold was a quiet sort of chap. But he was clever — quite brilliant, I believe. What they call a first-class financial brain. He was quite high up in the Treasury, you know."

"So I have heard."

"He read a good deal. And he collected stamps. And he was extremely fond of music.

He didn't dance, or care much for going out."

"Was it, do you think, a happy marriage?"

Commander McLaren's answer did not come quickly. He seemed to be puzzling it out.

"That sort of thing's very hard to say. . . . Yes, I think they were happy. He was devoted to her in his quiet way. I'm sure she was fond of him. They weren't likely to split up, if that's what you're thinking. They hadn't, perhaps, a lot in common."

Poirot nodded. It was as much as he was likely to get. He said: "Now tell me about that last evening. Mr. Clayton dined with you at the club. What did he say?"

"Told me he'd got to go to Scotland. Seemed vexed about it. We didn't have dinner, by the way. No time. Just sandwiches and a drink. For him, that is. I had only the drink. I was going out to a buffet supper, remember."

"Mr. Clayton mentioned a telegram?"

"Yes."

"He did not actually show you the telegram?"

"No."

"Did he say he was going to call on Rich?"

"Not definitely. In fact he said he doubted if he'd have time. He said, 'Margharita can explain or you can,' And then he said, 'See she gets home all right, won't you?' Then he went off. It was all quite natural and easy."

"He had no suspicion at all that the telegram wasn't genuine?"

"Wasn't it?" Commander McLaren looked startled.

"Apparently not."

"How very odd. . . ." Commander McLaren went into a kind of coma, emerging suddenly to say:

"But that really *is* odd. I mean, what's the point? Why should anybody *want* him to go to Scotland?"

"It is a question that needs answering, certainly."

Hercule Poirot left, leaving the commander apparently still puzzling on the matter.

The Spences lived in a minute house in Chelsea.

Linda Spence received Poirot with the utmost delight.

"Do tell me," she said. "Tell me *all* about Margharita! Where is she?"

"That I am not at liberty to state, madame."

"She *has* hidden herself well! Margharita is very clever at that sort of thing. But she'll be called to give evidence at the trial, I suppose? She can't wiggle herself out of that."

Poirot looked at her appraisingly. He decided grudgingly that she was attractive in the modern style (which at that moment resembled an underfed orphan child). It was not a type he admired. The artistically disordered hair fluffed out round her head, a pair of shrewd eyes watched him from a slightly dirty face devoid of makeup save for a vivid cerise mouth. She wore an enormous pale yellow sweater hanging almost to her knees, and tight black trousers.

"What's your part in all this?" demanded Mrs. Spence. "Get the boyfriend out of it somehow? Is that it? What a hope!"

"You think then, that he is guilty?"

"Of course. Who else?"

That, Poirot thought, was very much the question. He parried it by asking another question.

"What did Major Rich seem like to you on that fatal evening? As usual? Or not as usual?"

Linda Spence screwed up her eyes judicially.

"No, he wasn't himself. He was — different."

"How, different?"

"Well, surely, if you've just stabbed a man

in cold blood —"

"But you were not aware at the time that he had just stabbed a man in cold blood, were you?"

"No, of course not."

"So how did you account for his being 'different.' In what way?"

"Well — *distrait*. Oh, I don't know. But thinking it over afterwards I decided that there had definitely been *something*."

Poirot sighed.

"Who arrived first?"

"We did, Jim and I. And then Jock. And finally Margharita."

"When was Mr. Clayton's departure for Scotland first mentioned?"

"When Margharita came. She said to Charles: 'Arnold's terribly sorry. He's had to rush off to Edinburgh by the night train.' And Charles said: 'Oh, that's too bad.' And then Jock said: 'Sorry. Thought you already knew.' And then we had drinks."

"Major Rich at no time mentioned seeing Mr. Clayton that evening? He said nothing of his having called in on his way to the station?"

"Not that I heard."

"It was strange, was it not," said Poirot, "about that telegram?"

"What was strange?"

"It was a fake. Nobody in Edinburgh knows anything about it."

"So that's it. I wondered at the time."

"You have an idea about the telegram?"

"I should say it rather leaps to the eye."

"How do you mean exactly?"

"My dear man," said Linda. "Don't play the innocent. Unknown hoaxer gets the husband out of the way! For that night, at all events, the coast is clear."

"You mean that Major Rich and Mrs. Clayton planned to spend the night together."

"You have heard of such things, haven't you?" Linda looked amused.

"And the telegram was sent by one or the other of them?"

"It wouldn't surprise me."

"Major Rich and Mrs. Clayton were having an affair together you think?"

"Let's say I shouldn't be surprised if they were. I don't know it for a fact."

"Did Mr. Clayton suspect?"

"Arnold was an extraordinary person. He was all bottled up, if you know what I mean. I think he *did* know. But he was the kind of man who would never have let on. Anyone would think he was a dry stick with no feelings at all. But I'm pretty sure he wasn't like that underneath. The queer thing is that I should have been much less surprised if Arnold had stabbed Charles than the other way about. I've an idea Arnold was really an insanely jealous person."

"That is interesting."

"Though it's more likely, really, that he'd have done in Margharita. *Othello* — that sort of thing. Margharita, you know, has an extraordinary effect on men."

"She is a good-looking woman," said Poirot with judicious understatement.

"It was more than that. She *had* something. She would get men all het up — mad about her — and turn round and look at them with a sort of wide-eyed surprise that drove them barmy."

"Une femme fatale."

"That's probably the foreign name for it."

"You know her well?"

"My dear, she's one of my best friends — and I wouldn't trust her an inch!"

"Ah," said Poirot and shifted the subject to Commander McLaren.

"Jock? Old faithful? He's a pet. Born to be the friend of the family. He and Arnold were really close friends. I think Arnold unbent to him more than to anyone else. And of course he was Margharita's tame cat. He'd been devoted to her for years."

"And was Mr. Clayton jealous of him, too?"

"Jealous of Jock? What an idea! Margharita's genuinely fond of Jock, but she's never given him a thought of that kind. I don't think, really, that one ever would. . . . I don't know why. . . . It seems a shame. He's so nice."

Poirot switched to consideration of the valet. But beyond saying vaguely that he mixed a very good side-car, Linda Spence seemed to have no ideas about Burgess, and indeed seemed barely to have noticed him.

But she was quite quick in the uptake.

"You're thinking, I suppose, that *he* could have killed Arnold just as easily as Charles could? It seems to me madly unlikely."

"That remark depresses me, madame. But then, it seems to me (though you will probably not agree) that it is madly unlikely — not that Major Rich should kill Arnold Clayton — but that he should kill him in just the way he did."

"Stiletto stuff? Yes, definitely not in character. More likely the blunt instrument. Or he might have strangled him, perhaps?"

Poirot sighed.

"We are back at *Othello*. Yes, *Othello* . . . you have given me there a little idea. . . ."

"Have I? What —" There was the sound

of a latch-key and an opening door. "Oh, here's Jeremy. Do you want to talk to him, too?"

Jeremy Spence was a pleasant looking man of thirty-odd, well groomed, and almost ostentatiously discreet. Mrs. Spence said that she had better go and have a look at a casserole in the kitchen and went off, leaving the two men together.

Jeremy Spence displayed none of the engaging candor of his wife. He was clearly disliking very much being mixed up in the case at all, and his remarks were carefully noninformative. They had known the Claytons some time, Rich not so well. Had seemed a pleasant fellow. As far as he could remember, Rich had seemed absolutely as usual on the evening in question. Clayton and Rich always seemed on good terms. The whole thing seemed quite unaccountable.

Throughout the conversation Jeremy Spence was making it clear that he expected Poirot to take his departure. He was civil, but only just so.

"I am afraid," said Poirot, "that you do not like these questions?"

"Well, we've had quite a session of this with the police. I rather feel that's enough. We've told all we know or saw. Now — I'd like to forget it."

"You have my sympathy. It is most unpleasant to be mixed up in this. To be asked not only what you know or what you saw but perhaps even what you think?"

"Best not to think."

"But can one avoid it? Do you think, for instance, that Mrs. Clayton was in it, too? Did she plan the death of her husband with Rich?"

"Good lord, no." Spence sounded shocked and dismayed. "I'd no idea that there was any question of such a thing?"

"Has your wife not suggested such a possibility?"

"Oh Linda! You know what women are — always got their knife into each other. Margharita never gets much of a show from her own sex — a darned sight too attractive. But surely this theory about Rich and Margharita planning murder — that's fantastic!"

"Such things have been known. The weapon, for instance. It is the kind of weapon a woman might possess, rather than a man."

"Do you mean the police have traced it to her — They can't have! I mean —"

"I know nothing," said Poirot truthfully, and escaped hastily.

From the consternation on Spence's face, he judged that he had left that gentleman something to think about!

"You will forgive my saying, M. Poirot, that I cannot see how you can be of assistance to me in any way."

Poirot did not answer. He was looking thoughtfully at the man who had been charged with the murder of his friend Arnold Clayton.

He was looking at the firm jaw, the narrow head. A lean brown man, athletic and sinewy. Something of the greyhound about him. A man whose face gave nothing away, and who was receiving his visitor with a marked lack of cordiality.

"I quite understand that Mrs. Clayton sent you to see me with the best intentions. But quite frankly, I think she was unwise. Unwise both for her own sake and mine."

"You mean?"

Rich gave a nervous glance over his shoulder. But the attendant warder was the regulation distance away. Rich lowered his voice.

"They've got to find a motive for this ridiculous accusation. They'll try to bring that there was an — association between Mrs. Clayton and myself. That, as I know Mrs. Clayton will have told you, is quite untrue. We are friends, nothing more. But surely it is advisable that she should make no move on my behalf?"

Hercule Poirot ignored the point. Instead he picked out a word.

"You said this 'ridiculous' accusation. But it is not that, you know."

"I did *not* kill Arnold Clayton."

"Call it then a false accusation. Say the accusation is not true. But it is not *ridiculous*. On the contrary, it is highly plausible. You must know that very well."

"I can only tell you that to me it seems fantastic."

"Saying that will be of very little use to you. We must think of something more useful than that."

"I am represented by solicitors. They have briefed, I understand, eminent counsel to appear for my defence. I cannot accept your use of the word 'we.' "

Unexpectedly Poirot smiled.

"Ah," he said, in his most foreign manner, "that is the flea in the ear you give me. Very well. I go. I wanted to see you. I have seen you. Already I have looked up your career. You passed high up into Sandhurst. You passed into the Staff College. And so on and so on. I have made my own judgement of you today. You are not a stupid man."

"And what has all that got to do with it?"

"Everything! It is impossible that a man of your ability should commit a murder in the way this one was committed. Very well. You are innocent. Tell me now about your man-servant Burgess."

"Burgess?"

"Yes. If you didn't kill Clayton, Burgess must have done so. The conclusion seems inescapable. But why? There must *be* a 'why?' You are the only person who knows Burgess well enough to make a guess at it. Why, Major Rich, why?"

"I can't imagine. I simply can't see it. Oh, I've followed the same line of reasoning as you have. Yes, Burgess had opportunity — the only person who had except myself. The trouble is, I just can't believe it. Burgess is not the sort of man you can imagine murdering anybody."

"What do your legal advisers think?"

Rich's lips set in a grim line.

"My legal advisers spend their time asking me, in a persuasive way, if it isn't true that I have suffered all my life from blackouts when I don't really know what I am doing!"

"As bad as that," said Poirot. "Well, perhaps we shall find it is Burgess who is subject to blackouts. It is always an idea. The weapon now. They showed it to you and asked you if it was yours?"

"It was not mine. I had never seen it before."

"It was not yours, no. But are you quite sure you had never seen it before?"

"No." Was there a faint hesitation. "It's a kind of ornamental toy — really — One sees things like that lying about in people's houses."

"In a woman's drawing room, perhaps. Perhaps in Mrs. Clayton's drawing room?"

"Certainly NOT!"

The last word came out loudly and the warder looked up.

"*Très bien.* Certainly not — and there is no need to shout. But somewhere, at some time, you *have* seen something very like it. Eh? I am right?"

"I do not think so. . . . In some curio shop . . . perhaps."

"Ah, very likely." Poirot rose. "I take my leave."

"And now," said Hercule Poirot, "for Burgess. Yes, at long last, for Burgess."

He had learned something about the people in the case, from themselves and from each other. But nobody had given him any knowledge of Burgess. No clue, no hint, of what kind of a man he was.

When he saw Burgess he realized why.

The valet was waiting for him at Major Rich's flat, apprised of his arrival by a telephone call from Commander McLaren.

"I am M. Hercule Poirot."

"Yes, sir, I was expecting you."

Burgess held back the door with a deferential hand and Poirot entered. A small square entrance hall, a door on the left, open, leading into the sitting room. Burgess relieved Poirot of his hat and coat, and followed him into the sitting room.

"Ah," said Poirot looking round. "It was here, then, that it happened?"

"Yes, sir."

A quiet fellow, Burgess, white faced, a little weedy. Awkward shoulders and elbows. A flat voice with a provincial accent that Poirot did not know. From the east coast, perhaps. Rather a nervous man, perhaps — but otherwise no definite characteristics. It was hard to associate him with positive action of any kind. Could one postulate a negative killer?

He had those pale blue, rather shifty eyes that unobservant people often equate with dishonesty. Yet a liar can look you in the face with a bold and confident eye.

"What is happening to the flat?" Poirot inquired.

"I'm still looking after it, sir. Major Rich

arranged for my pay and to keep it nice until
— until —"

The eyes shifted uncomfortably.

"Until —" agreed Poirot.

He added in a matter-of-fact manner: "I should say that Major Rich will almost certainly be committed for trial. The case will come up probably within three months."

Burgess shook his head, not in denial, simply in perplexity.

"It really doesn't seem possible," he said.

"That Major Rich should be a murderer?"

"The whole thing. That chest —"

His eyes went across the room.

"Ah, so that is the famous chest?"

It was a mammoth piece of furniture of very dark polished wood, studded with brass, with a great brass hasp and antique lock.

"A handsome affair." Poirot went over to it.

It stood against the wall near the window, next to a modern cabinet for holding records. On the other side of it was a door, half ajar. The door was partly masked by a big painted leather screen.

"That leads into Major Rich's bedroom," said Burgess.

Poirot nodded. His eyes traveled to the other side of the room. There were two stereophonic record players, each on a low table, trailing snakelike electrical cord. There were easy chairs — a big table. On the walls were a set of Japanese prints. It was a handsome room, comfortable, but not luxurious.

He looked back at William Burgess.

"The discovery," he said kindly, "must have been a great shock to you."

"Oh it was, sir. I'll never forget it." The valet rushed into speech. Words poured from him. He felt, perhaps, that by telling the story often enough, he might at last expunge it from his mind.

"I'd gone round the room, sir. Clearing up. Glasses and so on. I'd just stooped to pick up a couple of olives off the floor — and I saw it — on the rug, a rusty dark stain. No, the rug's gone now. To the cleaners. The police had done with it. Whatever's that? I thought. Saying to myself, almost in joke like: 'Really it might be blood! But where does it come from? What got spilled?' And then I saw it was from the chest — down the side, here, where there's a crack. And I said, still not thinking anything, 'Well whatever — ?' And I lifted up the lid like this" (he suited the action to the word) "and there it was — the body of a man lying on his side doubled up — like he might be asleep. And that nasty foreign knife or dagger thing sticking up out of his neck. I'll never forget it —

never! Not as long as I live! The shock — not expecting it, you understand. . . ."

He breathed deeply.

"I let the lid fall and I ran out of the flat and down to the street. Looking for a policeman — and lucky, I found one — just round the corner."

Poirot regarded him reflectively. The performance, if it was a performance, was very good. He began to be afraid that it was not a performance — that it was just how things had happened.

"You did not think of awakening first Major Rich?" he asked.

"It never occurred to me, sir. What with the shock. I — I just wanted to get out of here —" he swallowed "and — and get help."

Poirot nodded.

"Did you realize that it was Mr. Clayton?" he asked.

"I ought to have, sir, but you know, I don't believe I did. Of course, as soon as I got back with the police officer, I said: 'Why, it's Mr. Clayton!' And he says: 'Who's Mr. Clayton?' And I says: 'He was here last night.' "

"Ah," said Poirot, "last night. . . . Do you remember exactly when it was Mr. Clayton arrived here?"

"Not to the minute. But as near as not a

234

quarter to eight, I'd say. . . ."

"You knew him well?"

"He and Mrs. Clayton had been here quite frequently during the year and a half I've been employed here."

"Did he seem quite as usual?"

"I think so. A little out of breath — but I took it he'd been hurrying. He was catching a train, or so he said."

"He had a bag with him, I suppose, as he was going to Scotland?"

"No, sir. I imagine he was keeping a taxi down below."

"Was he disappointed to find that Major Rich was out?"

"Not to notice. Just said he'd scribble a note. He came in here and went over to the desk and I went back to the kitchen. I was a little behindhand with the anchovy eggs. The kitchen's at the end of the passage and you don't hear very well from there. I didn't hear him go out or the master come in — but then I wouldn't expect to."

"And the next thing?"

"Major Rich called me. He was standing in the door here. He said he'd forgotten Mrs. Spence's Turkish cigarettes. I was to hurry out and get them. So I did. I brought them back and put them on the table in here. Of course I took it that Mr. Clayton had left by then to get his train."

"And nobody else came to the flat during the time Major Rich was out and you were in the kitchen?"

"No, sir — no one."

"Can you be sure of that?"

"How could anyone, sir? They'd have had to ring the bell."

Poirot shook his head. How could anyone? The Spences and McLaren and also Mrs. Clayton could, he already knew, account for every minute of their time. McLaren had been with acquaintances at the club, the Spences had had a couple of friends in for a drink before starting. Margharita Clayton had talked to a friend on the telephone at just that period. Not that he thought of any of them as possibilities. There would have been better ways of killing Arnold Clayton than following him to a flat with a manservant there and the host returning any moment. No, he had had a last minute hope of a "mysterious stranger"! Someone out of Clayton's apparently impeccable past, recognizing him in the street, following him here. Attacking him with the stiletto, thrusting the body into the chest, and fleeing. Pure melodrama, unrelated to reason or to probabilities! In tune with romantic historical fictions — matching the Spanish chest.

He went back across the room to the chest. He raised the lid. It came up easily, noiselessly.

In a faint voice, Burgess said: "It's been scrubbed out, sir, I saw to that."

Poirot bent over it. With a faint exclamation he bent lower. He explored with his fingers.

"These holes — at the back and one side — they look — they feel, as though they had been made quite recently."

"Holes, sir?" The valet bent to see. "I really couldn't say. I've never noticed them particularly."

"They are not very obvious. But they are there. What is their purpose, would you say?"

"I really wouldn't know, sir. Some animal, perhaps — I mean a beetle, something of that kind. Something that gnaws wood?"

"Some animal?" said Poirot. "I wonder."

He stepped back across the room.

"When you came in here with the cigarettes, was there anything at all about this room that looked different? Anything at all? Chairs moved, table, something of that kind?"

"It's odd your saying that, sir. . . . Now you come to mention it, there was. That screen there that cuts off the draft from the bedroom door, it was moved over a bit more to the left."

"Like this?" Poirot moved swiftly.

"A little more still. . . . That's right."

The screen had already masked about half of the chest. The way it was now arranged, it almost hid the chest altogether.

"Why did you think it had been moved?"

"I didn't think, sir."

(Another Miss Lemon!)

Burgess added doubtfully:

"I suppose it leaves the way into the bedroom clearer — if the ladies wanted to leave their wraps."

"Perhaps. But there might be another reason." Burgess looked inquiring. "The screen hides the chest now, and it hides the rug below the chest. If Major Rich stabbed Mr. Clayton, blood would presently start dripping through the cracks at the base of the chest. Someone might notice — as you noticed the next morning. So — the screen was moved."

"I never thought of that, sir."

"What are the lights like here, strong or dim?"

"I'll show you, sir."

Quickly, the valet drew the curtains and switched on a couple of lamps. They gave a soft mellow light, hardly strong enough even to read by. Poirot glanced up at a ceiling light.

"That wasn't on, sir. It's very little used."

Poirot looked round in the soft glow.

The valet said:

"I don't believe you'd see any bloodstains, sir, it's too dim."

"I think you are right. So, then, why was the screen moved?"

Burgess shivered.

"It's awful to think of — a nice gentleman like Major Rich doing a thing like that."

"You've no doubt that he did do it? Why did he do it, Burgess?"

"Well, he'd been through the war, of course. He might have had a head wound, mightn't he? They do say as sometimes it all flares up years afterwards. They suddenly go all queer and don't know what they're doing. And they say as often as not, it's their nearest and dearest as they goes for. Do you think it could have been like that?"

Poirot gazed at him. He sighed. He turned away.

"No," he said, "it was not like that."

With the air of a conjuror, a piece of crisp paper was insinuated into Burgess's hand.

"Oh thank you, sir, but really I don't —"

"You have helped me," said Poirot. "By showing me this room. By showing me what is in the room. By showing me what took place that evening. The impossible is never impossible! Remember that. I said that there were only two possibilities — I was wrong. There is a third possibility." He looked round the room again and gave a little shiver. "Pull back the curtains. Let in the light and the air. This room needs it. It needs cleansing. It will be a long time, I think, before it is purified from what afflicts it — the lingering memory of hate."

Burgess, his mouth open, handed Poirot his hat and coat. He seemed bewildered. Poirot, who enjoyed making incomprehensible statements, went down to the street with a brisk step.

When Poirot got home, he made a telephone call to Inspector Miller.

"What happened to Clayton's bag? His wife said he had packed one."

"It was at the club. He left it with the porter. Then he must have forgotten it and gone off without it."

"What was in it?"

"What you'd expect. Pyjamas, extra shirt, washing things."

"Very thorough."

"What did you expect would be in it?"

Poirot ignored that question. He said:

"About the stiletto. I suggest that you get hold of whatever cleaning woman attends Mrs. Spence's house. Find out if she ever saw anything like it lying about there."

"Mrs. Spence?" Miller whistled. "Is that the way your mind is working? The Spences were shown the stiletto. They didn't recognize it."

"Ask them again."

"Do you mean —"

"And then let me know what they say —"

"I can't imagine what you think you have got hold of!"

"Read *Othello*, Miller. Consider the characters in *Othello*. We've missed out one of them."

He rang off. Next he dialed Lady Chatterton. The number was engaged.

He tried again a little later. Still no success. He called for George, his valet, and instructed him to continue ringing the number until he got a reply. Lady Chatterton, he knew, was an incorrigible telephoner.

He sat down in a chair, carefully eased off his patent leather shoes, stretched his toes, and leaned back.

"I am old," said Hercule Poirot. "I tire easily. . . ." He brightened. "But the cells — they still function. Slowly — but they function. . . . *Othello*, yes. Who was it said that to me? Ah yes, Mrs. Spence. The bag . . . the screen . . . the body, lying there like a man asleep. A clever murder. Premeditated, planned . . . I think, *enjoyed!* . . ."

George announced to him that Lady Chatterton was on the line.

"Hercule Poirot here, madame. May I speak to your guest?"

"Why, of course! Oh M. Poirot, have you done something wonderful?"

"Not yet," said Poirot. "But possibly, it marches."

Presently Margharita's voice — quiet, gentle.

"Madame, when I asked you if you noticed anything out of place that evening at the party, you frowned, as though you remembered something — and then it escaped you. Would it have been the position of the screen that night?"

"The screen? Why, of course, yes. It was not quite in its usual place."

"Did you dance that night?"

"Part of the time."

"Who did you dance with mostly?"

"Jeremy Spence. He's a wonderful dancer. Charles is good but not spectacular. He and Linda danced, and now and then we changed. Jock McLaren doesn't dance. He got out the records and sorted them and arranged what we'd have."

"You had serious music later?"

"Yes."

There was a pause. Then Margharita said:

"M. Poirot, what is — all this? Have you — is there — *hope?*"

"Do you ever know, madame, what the people around you are feeling?"

Her voice, faintly surprised, said:

"I — suppose so."

"I suppose not. I think you have no idea. I think that is the tragedy of your life. But the tragedy is for other people — not for you.

"Someone today mentioned to me *Othello*. I asked you if your husband was jealous, and you said you thought he must be. But you said it quite lightly. You said it as Desdemona might have said it, not realizing danger. She, too, recognized jealousy, but she did not understand it, because she herself never had, and never could, experience jealousy. She was, I think, quite unaware of the force of acute physical passion. She loved her husband with the romantic fervor of hero worship, she loved her friend Cassio, quite innocently, as a close companion. . . . I think that because of her immunity to passion, she herself drove men mad. . . . Am I making sense to you, madame?"

There was a pause — and then Margharita's voice answered. Cool, sweet, a little bewildered:

"I don't — I don't really understand what you are saying. . . ."

Poirot sighed. He spoke in matter-of-fact tones.

"This evening," he said, "I pay you a visit."

Inspector Miller was not an easy man to persuade. But equally Hercule Poirot was not an easy man to shake off until he had got his way. Inspector Miller grumbled, but capitulated.

"— though what Lady Chatterton's got to do with this —"

"Nothing, really. She has provided asylum for a friend, that is all."

"About those Spences — how did you know?"

"That stiletto came from there? It was a mere guess. Something Jeremy Spence said gave me the idea. I suggested that the stiletto belonged to Margharita Clayton. He showed that he knew positively that it did *not*." He paused. "What did they say?" he asked with some curiosity.

"Admitted that it was very like a toy dagger they'd once had. But it had been mislaid some weeks ago, and they had really forgotten about it. I suppose Rich pinched it from there."

"A man who likes to play safe, Mr. Jeremy Spence," said Hercule Poirot. He muttered to himself: "Some weeks ago. . . . Oh yes, the planning began a long time ago."

"Eh, what's that?"

"We arrive," said Poirot. The taxi drew up at Lady Chatterton's house in Cheriton Street. Poirot paid the fare.

Margharita Clayton was waiting for them in the room upstairs. Her face hardened when she saw Miller.

"I didn't know —"

"You did not know who the friend was I proposed to bring?"

"Inspector Miller is not a friend of mine."

"That rather depends on whether you want to see justice done or not, Mrs. Clayton. Your husband was murdered —"

"And now we have to talk of who killed him," said Poirot quickly. "May we sit down, madame?"

Slowly Margharita sat down in a high-backed chair facing the two men.

"I ask," said Poirot, addressing both his hearers, "to listen to me patiently. I think I now know what happened on that fatal evening at Major Rich's flat. . . . We started, all of us, by an assumption that was not true —

the assumption that there were only two persons who had the opportunity of putting the body in the chest — that is to say, Major Rich or William Burgess. But we were wrong — there was a third person at the flat that evening who had an equally good opportunity to do so."

"And who was that?" demanded Miller skeptically. "The lift boy?"

"No. *Arnold Clayton.*"

"What? Concealed his own dead body? You're crazy."

"Naturally not a dead body — a live one. In simple terms, he hid himself in the chest. A thing that has often been done throughout the course of history. The dead bride in the *Mistletoe Bough*, Iachimo with designs on the virtue of Imogen, and so on. I thought of it as soon as I saw that there had been holes bored in the chest quite recently. Why? They were made so that there might be a sufficiency of air in the chest. Why was the screen moved from its usual position that evening? So as to hide the chest from the people in the room. So that the hidden man could lift the lid from time to time and relieve his cramp, and hear better what went on."

"But why," demanded Margharita wide-eyed with astonishment. "Why should Arnold want to hide in the chest?"

"Is it you who ask that, madame? Your husband was a jealous man. He was also an inarticulate man. 'Bottled up,' as your friend Mrs. Spence put it. His jealousy mounted. It tortured him! Were you or were you not Rich's mistress? He did not know! He *had* to know! So — a 'telegram from Scotland,' the telegram that was never sent and that no one ever saw! The overnight bag is packed and conveniently forgotten at the club. He goes to the flat at a time when he has probably ascertained Rich will be out. He tells the valet he will write a note. As soon as he is left alone, he bores the holes in the chest, moves the screen, and climbs inside the chest. Tonight he will know the truth. Perhaps his wife will stay behind the others, perhaps she will go but come back again. That night the desperate, jealousy-racked man will *know*. . . ."

"You're not saying he stabbed *himself?*" Miller's voice was incredulous. "Nonsense!"

"Oh no, someone else stabbed him. Somebody who knew he was there. It was murder all right. Carefully planned, long premeditated murder. Think of the other characters in *Othello*. It is Iago we should have remembered. Subtle poisoning of Arnold Clayton's mind; hints, suspicions. Honest Iago, the faithful friend, the man you always believe!

Arnold Clayton believed him. Arnold Clayton let his jealousy be played upon, be roused to fever pitch. Was the plan of hiding in the chest Arnold's own idea? He may have thought it was — probably he did think so! And so the scene is set. The stiletto, quietly abstracted some weeks earlier, is ready. The evening comes. The lights are low, the gramophone is playing, two couples dance, the odd man out is busy at the record cabinet, close to the Spanish chest and its masking screen. To slip behind the screen, lift the lid and strike — Audacious, but quiet easy!"

"Clayton would have cried out!"

"Not if he were drugged," said Poirot. "According to the valet, the body was 'lying like a man asleep.' Clayton was asleep, drugged by the only man who *could* have drugged him, the man he had had a drink with at the club."

"Jock?" Margharita's voice rose high in childlike surprise. "Jock? Not dear old Jock. Why, I've known Jock all my life! Why on earth should Jock . . . ?"

Poirot turned on her.

"Why did two Italians fight a duel? Why did a young man shoot himself? Jock McLaren is an inarticulate man. He has resigned himself, perhaps, to being the faithful friend to you and your husband, but then

248

comes Major Rich as well. It is too much! In the darkness of hate and desire, he plans what is well nigh the perfect murder — a double murder, for Rich is almost certain to be found guilty of it. And with Rich and your husband both out of the way — he thinks that at last you may turn to *him*. And perhaps, madame, you would have done. . . . Eh?"

She was staring at him, wide-eyed, horror-struck. . . .

Almost unconsciously she breathed:

"Perhaps . . . I don't know. . . ."

Inspector Miller spoke with sudden authority.

"This is all very well, Poirot. It's a theory, nothing more. There's not a shred of evidence. Probably not a word of it is true."

"It is all true."

"But there's no *evidence*. There's nothing we can act on."

"You are wrong. I think that McLaren, if this is put to him, will admit it. That is, if it is made clear to him that Margharita Clayton knows. . . ."

Poirot paused and added:

"Because, once he knows *that*, he has lost. . . . The perfect murder has been in vain."

IX

The Harlequin Tea Set

Mr. Satterthwaite clucked twice in vexation. Whether right in his assumption or not, he was more and more convinced that cars nowadays broke down far more frequently than they used to do. The only cars he trusted were old friends who had survived the test of time. They had their little idiosyncrasies, but you knew about those, provided for them, fulfilled their wants before the demand became too acute. But new cars! Full of new gadgets, different kinds of windows, an instrument panel newly and differently arranged, handsome in its glistening wood, but being unfamiliar, your groping hand hovered uneasily over fog lights, windshield wipers, the choke, et cetera. All these things with knobs in a place where you didn't expect them. And when your gleaming new purchase failed in performance, your local garage uttered the intensely irritating words: "Teething troubles. Splendid car, sir, these roadsters Super Superbos. All the latest accessories. But bound to have their teething troubles, you know. Ha, ha." Just as though a car was a baby.

But Mr. Satterthwaite, being now of an advanced age, was strongly of the opinion that a new car ought to be fully adult. Tested, inspected, and its teething troubles already dealt with before it came into its purchaser's possession.

Mr. Satterthwaite was on his way to pay a weekend visit to friends in the country. His new car had already, on the way from London, given certain symptoms of discomfort, and was now drawn up in a garage waiting for the diagnosis, and how long it would take before he could resume progress towards his destination. His chauffeur was in consultation with a mechanic. Mr. Satterthwaite sat, striving for patience. He had assured his hosts, on the telephone the night before, that he would be arriving in good time for tea. He would reach Doverton Kingsbourne, he assured them, well before four o'clock.

He clucked again in irritation and tried to turn his thoughts to something pleasant. It was no good sitting here in a state of acute irritation, frequently consulting his wrist-watch, clucking once more and giving, he had to realize, a very good imitation of a hen pleased with its prowess in laying an egg.

251

Yes. Something pleasant. Yes, now hadn't there been something — something he had noticed as they were driving along. Not very long ago. Something that he had seen through the window which had pleased and excited him. But before he had had time to think about it, the car's misbehavior had become more pronounced and a rapid visit to the nearest service station had been inevitable.

What was it that he had seen? On the left — no, on the right. Yes, on the right as they drove slowly through the village street. Next door to a post office. Yes, he was quite sure of that. Next door to a post office because the sight of the post office had given him the idea of telephoning to the Addisons to break the news that he might be slightly late in his arrival. The post office. A village post office. And next to it — yes, definitely, next to it, next door or if not next door the door after. Something that had stirred old memories, and he had wanted — just what was it that he had wanted? Oh dear, it would come to him presently. It was mixed up with a color. Several colors. Yes, a color or colors. Or a word. Some definite word that had stirred memories, thoughts, pleasures gone by, excitement, recalling something that had been vivid and alive. Something in which he himself had not only seen but observed. No, he had done more. He had taken part. Taken part in what, and why, and where? All sorts of places. The answer came quickly at the last thought. All sorts of places.

On an island? In Corsica? At Monte Carlo watching the croupier spinning his roulette wheel? A house in the country? All sorts of places. And he had been there, and someone else. Yes, someone else. It all tied up with that. He was getting there at last. If he could just . . . He was interrupted at that moment by the chauffeur coming to the window with the garage mechanic in tow behind him.

"Won't be long now, sir," the chauffeur assured Mr. Satterthwaite cheerfully. "Matter of ten minutes or so. Not more."

"Nothing seriously wrong," said the mechanic, in a low, hoarse, country voice. "Teething troubles, as you might say."

Mr. Satterthwaite did not cluck this time. He gnashed his own teeth. A phrase he had often read in books and which in old age he seemed to have got into the habit of doing himself, due, perhaps, to the slight looseness of his upper plate. Really, teething trouble! Toothache. Teeth gnashing. False teeth. One's whole life centered, he thought, about teeth.

"Doverton Kingsbourne's only a few miles

away," said the chauffeur, "and they've a taxi here. You could go on in that, sir, and I'd bring the car along later as soon as it's fixed up."

"No!" said Mr. Satterthwaite.

He said the word explosively, and both the chauffeur and the mechanic looked startled. Mr. Satterthwaite's eyes were sparkling. His voice was clear and decisive. Memory had come to him.

"I propose," he said, "to walk the road we have just come by. When the car is ready, you will pick me up there. The Harlequin Cafe, I think it is called."

"It's not very much of a place, sir," the mechanic advised.

"That is where I shall be," said Mr. Satterthwaite, speaking with a kind of regal autocracy.

He walked off briskly. The two men stared after him.

"Don't know what's got into him," said the chauffeur. "Never seen him like that before."

The village of Kingsbourne Ducis did not live up to the old world grandeur of its name. It was a smallish village consisting of one street. A few houses. Shops that were dotted rather unevenly, sometimes betraying the fact that they were houses which had been turned into shops or that they were shops which now existed as houses without any industrial intentions.

It was not particularly old world or beautiful. It was just simple and rather unobtrusive. Perhaps that was why, thought Mr. Satterthwaite, that a dash of brilliant color had caught his eye. Ah, here he was at the post office. The post office was a simply functioning post office with a pillar box outside, a display of some newspapers and some postcards, and surely, next to it, yes there was the sign up above. The Harlequin Cafe. A sudden qualm struck Mr. Satterthwaite. Really, he was getting too old. He had fancies. Why should that one word stir his heart? *The Harlequin Cafe.*

The mechanic at the service station had been quite right. It did not look like a place in which one would really be tempted to have a meal. A snack, perhaps. A morning coffee. Then why? But he suddenly realized why. Because the cafe, or perhaps one could better put it as the house that sheltered the cafe, was in two portions. One side of it had small tables with chairs round them arranged ready for patrons who came here to eat. But the other side was a shop. A shop that sold china. It was not an antique shop. It had no little shelves of glass vases or mugs. It was a shop that sold modern goods, and the show window that gave on the street was at the present moment housing every shade of the rainbow. A tea set of largish cups and saucers, each one of a different color. Blue, red, yellow, green, pink, purple. Really, Mr. Satterthwaite thought, a wonderful show of color. No wonder it had struck his eye as the car had passed slowly beside the pavement, looking ahead for any sign of a garage or a service station. It was labeled with a large card as "A Harlequin Tea Set."

It was the word "harlequin" of course which had remained fixed in Mr. Satterthwaite's mind, although just far enough back in his mind so that it had been difficult to recall it. The gay colors. The harlequin colors. And he had thought, wondered, had the absurd but exciting idea that in some way here was a call to him. To him specially. Here, perhaps, eating a meal or purchasing cups and saucers might be his own old friend, Mr. Harley Quin. How many years was it since he had last seen Mr. Quin? A large number of years. Was it the day he had seen Mr. Quin walking away from him down a country lane, Lovers' Lane they had called it? He had always expected to see Mr. Quin again, once a year at least. Possibly twice a year. But no. That had not happened.

And so today he had had the wonderful and surprising idea that here, in the village of Kingsbourne Ducis, he might once again find Mr. Harley Quin.

"Absurd of me," said Mr. Satterthwaite, "quite absurd of me. Really, the ideas one has as one gets old!"

He had missed Mr. Quin. Missed something that had been one of the most exciting things in the late years of his life. Someone who might turn up anywhere and who, if he did turn up, was always an announcement that something was going to happen. Something that was going to happen to him. No, that was not quite right. Not *to* him, but through him. That was the exciting part. Just from the words that Mr. Quin might utter. Words. Things he might show him, ideas would come to Mr. Satterthwaite. He would see things, he would imagine things, he would find out things. He would deal with something that needed to be dealt with. And opposite him would sit Mr. Quin, perhaps smiling approval. Something that Mr. Quin said would start the flow of ideas, the active person would be he himself. He — Mr. Satterthwaite. The man with so many old friends. A man among whose friends had been duchesses, an occasional bishop, people that counted. Especially, he had to admit, people who had counted in the social world. Because, after all, Mr. Satterthwaite had always been a snob. He had liked duchesses, he had liked knowing old families, families who had represented the landed gentry of England for several generations. And he had had, too, an interest in young people not necessarily socially important. Young people who were in trouble, who were in love, who were unhappy, who needed help. Because of Mr. Quin, Mr. Satterthwaite was enabled to give help.

And now, like an idiot, he was looking into an unprepossessing village cafe and a shop for modern china and tea sets and casseroles, no doubt.

"All the same," said Mr. Satterthwaite to himself, "I must go in. Now I've been foolish enough to walk back here, I must go in just — well, just in case. They'll be longer, I expect, doing the car than they say. It will be more than ten minutes. Just in case there is anything interesting inside."

He looked once more at the window full of china. He appreciated suddenly that it was good china. Well made. A good modern product. He looked back into the past, remembering. The Duchess of Leith, he remembered. What a wonderful lady she had been. How kind she had been to her maid on the occasion of a very rough sea voyage to the island of Corsica. She had ministered to her with the kindliness of a ministering angel and only on the next day had she resumed her autocratic, bullying manner, which the domestics of those days had seemed able to stand quite easily without any sign of rebellion.

Maria. Yes, that's what the Duchess's name had been. Dear old Maria Leith. Ah well. She had died some years ago. But she had had a harlequin breakfast set, he remembered. Yes. Big round cups in different colors. Black. Yellow, red, and a particularly pernicious shade of puce. Puce, he thought, must have been a favorite color of hers. She had had a Rockingham tea set, he remembered, in which the predominating color had been puce decorated with gold.

"Ah," sighed Mr. Satterthwaite, "those were the days. Well, I suppose I'd better go in. Perhaps order a cup of coffee or something. It will be very full of milk, I expect, and possibly already sweetened. But still, one has to pass the time."

He went in. The cafe side was practically empty. It was early, Mr. Satterthwaite supposed, for people to want cups of tea. And anyway, very few people did want cups of tea nowadays. Except, that is, occasionally

259

elderly people in their own homes. There was a young couple in the far window and two women gossiping at a table against the back wall.

"I said to her," one of them was saying, "I said you can't do that sort of thing. No, it's not the sort of thing that I'll put up with, and I said the same to Henry and he agreed with me."

It shot through Mr. Satterthwaite's mind that Henry must have rather a hard life and that no doubt he had found it always wise to agree, whatever the proposition put up to him might be. A most unattractive woman with a most unattractive friend. He turned his attention to the other side of the building, murmuring, "May I just look round?"

There was quite a pleasant woman in charge and she said, "Oh yes, sir. We've got a good stock at present."

Mr. Satterthwaite looked at the colored cups, picked up one or two of them, examined the milk jug, picked up a china zebra and considered it, examined some ashtrays of a fairly pleasing pattern. He heard chairs being pushed back and turning his head, noted that the two middle-aged women still discussing former grievances had paid their bill and were now leaving the shop. As they went out of the door, a tall man in a dark suit came in. He sat down at the table which they had just vacated. His back was to Mr. Satterthwaite, who thought that he had an attractive back. Lean, strong, well-muscled but rather dark and sinister looking because there was very little light in the shop. Mr. Satterthwaite looked back again at the ashtrays. "I might buy an ashtray so as not to cause a disappointment to the shop owner," he thought. As he did so, the sun came out suddenly.

He had not realized that the shop had looked dim because of the lack of sunshine. The sun must have been under a cloud for some time. It had clouded over, he remembered, at about the time they had got to the service station. But now there was this sudden burst of sunlight. It caught up the colors of the china and through a colored glass window of somewhat ecclesiastical pattern which must, Mr. Satterthwaite thought, have been left over from the original Victorian house. The sun came through the window and lit up the dingy cafe. In some curious way it lit up the back of the man who had just sat down there. Instead of a dark black silhouette, there was now a festoon of colors. Red and blue and yellow. And suddenly Mr. Satterthwaite realized that he was looking at exactly what he had hoped to find. His intuition had not played him false. He knew who it was who had just come in and sat down there. He knew so well that he had no need to wait until he could look at the face. He turned his back on the china, went back into the cafe, round the corner of the round table and sat down opposite the man who had just come in.

"Mr. Quin," said Mr. Satterthwaite. "I knew somehow it was going to be you."

Mr. Quin smiled.

"You always know so many things," he said.

"It's a long time since I've seen you," said Mr. Satterthwaite.

"Does time matter?" said Mr. Quin.

"Perhaps not. You may be right. Perhaps not."

"May I offer you some refreshment?"

"Is there any refreshment to be had?" said Mr. Satterthwaite doubtfully. "I suppose you must have come in for that purpose."

"One is never quite sure of one's purpose, is one?" said Mr. Quin.

"I am so pleased to see you again," said Mr. Satterthwaite. "I'd almost forgotten, you know. I mean forgotten the way you talk, the things you say. The things you make me think of, the things you make me do."

"I — make you do? You are so wrong.

You have always known yourself just what you wanted to do and why you want to do it and why you know so well that they have to be done."

"I only feel that when you are here."

"Oh no," said Mr. Quin lightly. "I have nothing to do with it. I am just — as I've often told you — I am just passing by. That is all."

"Today you are passing by through Kingsbourne Ducis."

"And you are not passing by. You are going to a definite place. Am I right?"

"I am going to see a very old friend. A friend I have not seen for a good many years. He's old now. Somewhat crippled. He has had one stroke. He has recovered from it quite well, but one never knows."

"Does he live by himself?"

"Not now, I am glad to say. His family have come back from abroad, what is left of his family that is. They have been living with him now for some months. I am glad to be able to come and see them again all together. Those, that's to say, that I have seen before, and those that I have not seen."

"You mean children?"

"Children and grandchildren." Mr. Satterthwaite sighed. Just for a moment he was sad that he had had no children and no grandchildren and no great-grandchildren himself. He did not usually regret it at all.

"They have some special Turkish coffee here," said Mr. Quin. "Really good of its kind. Everything else is, as you have guessed, rather unpalatable. But one can always have a cup of Turkish coffee, can one not? Let us have one because I suppose you will soon have to get on with your pilgrimage, or whatever it is."

In the doorway came a small black dog. He came and sat down by the table and looked up at Mr. Quin.

"Your dog?" said Mr. Satterthwaite.

"Yes. Let me introduce you to Hermes." He stroked the black dog's head. "Coffee," he said. "Tell Ali."

The black dog walked from the table through a door at the back of the shop. They heard him give a short, incisive bark. Presently he reappeared and with him came a young man with a very dark complexion, wearing an emerald green pullover.

"Coffee, Ali," said Mr. Quin. "Two coffees."

"Turkish coffee. That's right, isn't it, sir?" He smiled and disappeared.

The dog sat down again.

"Tell me," said Mr. Satterthwaite, "tell me where you've been and what you have been doing and why I have not seen you for so long."

"I have just told you that time really means nothing. It is clear in my mind and I think it is clear in yours the occasion when we last met."

"A very tragic occasion," said Mr. Satterthwaite. "I do not really like to think of it."

"Because of death? But death is not always a tragedy. I have told you that before."

"No," said Mr. Satterthwaite, "perhaps that death — the one we are both thinking of — was not a tragedy. But all the same . . ."

"But all the same it is life that really matters. You are quite right, of course," said Mr. Quin. "Quite right. It is life that matters. We do not want someone young, someone who is happy, or could be happy, to die. Neither of us wants that, do we. That is the reason why we must always save a life when the command comes."

"Have you got a command for me?"

"Me — command for you?" Harley Quin's long, sad face brightened into its peculiarly charming smile. "I have no commands for *you*, Mr. Satterthwaite. I have never had commands. You yourself know things, see things, know what to do, do them. It has nothing to do with me."

"Oh yes, it has," said Mr. Satterthwaite. "You're not going to change my mind on that point. But tell me. Where have you been during what it is too short to call time?"

"Well, I have been here and there. In different countries, different climates, different adventures. But mostly, as usual, just passing by. I think it is more for you to tell me not only what you have been doing but what you are going to do now. More about where you are going. Who you are going to meet. Your friends, what they are like."

"Of course I will tell you. I should enjoy telling you because I have been wondering, thinking you know about these friends I am going to. When you have not seen a family for a long time, when you have not been closely connected with them for many years, it is always a nervous moment when you are going to resume old friendships and old ties."

"You are so right," said Mr. Quin.

The Turkish coffee was brought in little cups of oriental pattern. All placed them with a smile and departed. Mr. Satterthwaite sipped approvingly.

"As sweet as love, as black as night and as hot as hell. That is the old Arab phrase, isn't it?"

Harley smiled over his shoulder and nodded.

266

"Yes," said Mr. Satterthwaite, "I must tell you where I am going, though what I am doing hardly matters. I am going to renew old friendships, to make acquaintance with the younger generation. Tom Addison, as I have said, is a very old friend of mine. We did many things together in our young days. Then, as often happens, life parted us. He was in the Diplomatic Service, went abroad for several foreign posts in turn. Sometimes I went and stayed with him, sometimes I saw him when he was home in England. One of his early posts was in Spain. He married a Spanish girl, a very beautiful, dark girl called Pilar. He loved her very much."

"They had children?"

"Two daughters. A fair-haired baby like her father, called Lily, and a second daughter, Maria, who took after her Spanish mother. I was Lily's godfather. Naturally, I did not see either of the children very often. Two or three times a year I either gave a party for Lily or went to see her at her school. She was a sweet and lovely person. Very devoted to her father and he was very devoted to her. But in between these meetings, these revivals of friendship, we went through some difficult times. You will know about it as well as I do. I and my contemporaries had difficulties in meeting through the war years.

Lily married a pilot in the Air Force. A fighter pilot. Until the other day I had even forgotten his name. Simon Gilliatt. Squadron Leader Gilliatt."

"He was killed in the war?"

"No, no. No. He came through safely. After the war he resigned from the Air Force and he and Lily went out to Kenya as so many did. They settled there and they lived very happily. They had a son, a little boy called Roland. Later when he was at school in England I saw him once or twice. The last time, I think, was when he was twelve years old. A nice boy. He had red hair like his father. I've not seen him since so I am looking forward to seeing him today. He is twenty-three — twenty-four now. Time goes on so."

"Is he married?"

"No. Well, not yet."

"Ah. Prospects of marriage?"

"Well, I wondered from something Tom Addison said in his letter. There is a girl cousin. The younger daughter, Maria, married the local doctor. I never knew her very well. It was rather sad. She died in childbirth. Her little girl was called Inez, a family name chosen by her Spanish grandmother. As it happens I have seen Inez only once since she grew up. A dark, Spanish type very much like her grandmother. But I am boring you with all this."

"No. I want to hear it. It is very interesting to me."

"I wonder why," said Mr. Satterthwaite.

He looked at Mr. Quin with that slight air of suspicion which sometimes came to him.

"You want to know all about this family. Why?"

"So that I can picture it, perhaps, in my mind."

"Well, this house I am going to, Doverton Kingsbourne it is called. It is quite a beautiful old house. Not so spectacular as to invite tourists or to be open to visitors on special days. Just a quiet country house to be lived in by an Englishman who has served his country and returns to enjoy a mellow life when the age of retirement comes. Tom was always fond of country life. He enjoyed fishing. He was a good shot and we had very happy days together in his family home of his boyhood. I spent many of my own holidays as a boy at Doverton Kingsbourne. And all through my life I have had that image in my mind. No place like Doverton Kingsbourne. No other house to touch it. Every time I drove near it I would make a detour and just pass to see the view through a gap in the trees of the long lane that runs in front of the house, glimpses of the river where we used to fish, and of the house itself. And I would remember all the things that Tom and I did together. He has been a man of action. A man who has done things. And I — I have just been an old bachelor."

"You have been more than that," said Mr. Quin. "You have been a man who made friends, who had many friends and who has served his friends well."

"Well, if I can think that. Perhaps you are being too kind."

"Not at all. You are very good company besides. The stories you can tell, the things you've seen, the places you have visited. The curious things that have happened in your life. You could write a whole book on them," said Mr. Quin.

"I should make you the main character in it if I did."

"No, you would not," said Mr. Quin. "I am the one who passes by. That is all. But go on. Tell me more."

"Well, this is just a family chronicle that I'm telling you. As I say, there were long periods, years of time when I did not see any of them. But they have been always my old friends. I saw Tom and Pilar until the time when Pilar died — she died rather young, unfortunately — Lily, my godchild; Inez, the quiet doctor's daughter, who lives in the village with her father. . . ."

"How old is the daughter?"

"Inez is nineteen or twenty, I think. I shall be glad to make friends with her."

"So it is on the whole a happy chronicle?"

"Not entirely. Lily, my godchild — the one who went to Kenya with her husband — was killed there in an automobile accident. She was killed outright, leaving behind her a baby of barely a year old, little Roland. Simon, her husband, was quite broken-hearted. They were an unusually happy couple. However, the best thing happened to him that could happen, I suppose. He married again, a young woman who was the widow of a squadron leader, a friend of his and who also had been left with a baby the same age. Little Timothy and little Roland had only two or three months in age between them. Simon's marriage, I believe, has been quite happy enough though I've not seen them, of course, because they continued to live in Kenya. The boys were brought up like brothers. They went to the same school in England and spent their holidays usually in Kenya. I have not seen them, of course, for many years. Well, you know what has happened in Kenya. Some people have managed to stay on. Some people, friends of mine, have gone to Western Australia and have settled again happily there with their families. Some have come home to this country.

"Simon Gilliatt and his wife and their two children left Kenya. It was not the same to them and so they came home and accepted the invitation that has always been given them and renewed every year by old Tom Addison. They have come, his son-in-law, his son-in-law's second wife, and the two children, now grown-up boys, or rather, young men. They have come to live as a family there and they are happy. Tom's other grandchild, Inez Horton, as I told you, lives in the village with her father, the doctor, and she spends a good deal of her time, I gather, at Doverton Kingsbourne with Tom Addison, who is very devoted to his granddaughter. They sound all very happy together there. He has urged me several times to come there and see. Meet them all again. And so I accepted the invitation. Just for a weekend. It will be sad in some ways to see dear old Tom again, somewhat crippled, with perhaps not a very long expectation of life but still cheerful and gay, as far as I can make out. And to see also the old house again. Doverton Kingsbourne. Tied up with all my boyish memories. When one has not lived a very eventful life, when nothing has happened to one personally, and that is true of me, the things that remain with you are the friends, the houses, and the things you did as a child and a boy and a young man. There is only one thing that worries me."

"You should not be worried. What is it that worries you?"

"That I might be — disappointed. The house one remembers, one has dreams of, when one might come to see it again it would not be as you remembered it or dreamed it. A new wing would have been added, the garden would have been altered, all sorts of things can have happened to it. It is a very long time, really, since I have been there."

"I think your memories will go with you," said Mr. Quin. "I am glad you are going there."

"I have an idea," said Mr. Satterthwaite. "Come with me. Come with me on this visit. You need not fear that you'll not be welcome. Dear Tom Addison is the most hospitable fellow in the world. Any friend of mine would immediately be a friend of his. Come with me. You must. I insist."

Making an impulsive gesture, Mr. Satterthwaite nearly knocked his coffee cup off the table. He caught it just in time.

At that moment the shop door was pushed open, ringing its old-fashioned bell as it did so. A middle-aged woman came in. She was slightly out of breath and looked somewhat hot. She was good-looking still, with a head of auburn hair only just touched here and there with grey. She had that clear ivory-colored skin that so often goes with reddish hair and blue eyes, and she had kept her figure well. The newcomer swept a quick glance round the cafe and turned immediately into the china shop.

"Oh!" she exclaimed, "you've still got some of the Harlequin cups."

"Yes, Mrs. Gilliatt, we had a new stock arrive in yesterday."

"Oh, I'm so pleased. I really have been very worried. I rushed down here. I took one of the boys' motorbikes. They'd gone off somewhere and I couldn't find either of them. But I really had to do something. There was an unfortunate accident this morning with some of the cups and we've got people arriving for tea and a party this afternoon. So if you can give me a blue and a green and perhaps I'd better have another red one as well in case. That's the worst of these different-colored cups, isn't it?"

"Well, I know they do say as it's a disadvantage and you can't always replace the particular color you want."

Mr. Satterthwaite's head had gone over his

shoulder now and he was looking with some interest at what was going on. Mrs. Gilliatt, the shop woman had said. But of course. He realized it now. This must be — he rose from his seat, half hesitating, and then took a step or two into the shop.

"Excuse me," he said, "but are you — are you Mrs. Gilliatt from Doverton Kingsbourne?"

"Oh yes. I am Beryl Gilliatt. Do you — I mean . . . ?"

She looked at him, wrinkling her brows a little. An attractive woman, Mr. Satterthwaite thought. Rather a hard face, perhaps, but competent. So this was Simon Gilliatt's second wife. She hadn't got the beauty of Lily, but she seemed an attractive woman, pleasant and efficient. Suddenly a smile came to Mrs. Gilliatt's face.

"I do believe . . . yes, of course. My father-in-law, Tom, has got a photograph of you and you must be the guest we are expecting this afternoon. You must be Mr. Satterthwaite."

"Exactly," said Mr. Satterthwaite. "That is who I am. But I shall have to apologize very much for being so much later in arriving than I said. But unfortunately my car has had a breakdown. It's in the garage now, being attended to."

"Oh, how miserable for you. But what a shame. But it's not tea time yet. Don't worry. We've put it off anyway. As you probably heard, I ran down to replace a few cups which unfortunately got swept off the table this morning. Whenever one has anyone to lunch or tea or dinner, something like that always happens."

"There you are, Mrs. Gilliatt," said the woman in the shop. "I'll wrap them up in here. Shall I put them in a box for you?"

"No, if you'll just put some paper around them and put them in this shopping bag of mine, they'll be quite all right that way."

"If you are returning to Doverton Kingsbourne," said Mr. Satterthwaite, "I could give you a lift in my car. It will be arriving from the garage any moment now."

"That's very kind of you. I wish really I could accept. But I've simply got to take the motorbike back. The boys will be miserable without it. They're going somewhere this evening."

"Let me introduce you," said Mr. Satterthwaite. He turned towards Mr. Quin, who had risen to his feet and was now standing quite near. "This is an old friend of mine, Mr. Harley Quin, whom I have just happened to run across here. I've been trying to persuade him to come along to Doverton

276

Kingsbourne. Would it be possible, do you think, for Tom to put up yet another guest for tonight?"

"Oh, I'm sure it would be quite all right," said Beryl Gilliatt. "I'm sure he'd be delighted to see another friend of yours. Perhaps it's a friend of his as well."

"No," said Mr. Quin, "I've never met Mr. Addison, though I've often heard my friend Mr. Satterthwaite speak of him."

"Well then, do let Mr. Satterthwaite bring you. We should be delighted."

"I am very sorry," said Mr. Quin. "Unfortunately, I have another engagement. Indeed" — he looked at his watch — "I must start for it immediately. I am late already, which is what comes of meeting old friends."

"Here you are, Mrs. Gilliatt," said the saleswoman. "It'll be quite all right, I think, in your bag."

Beryl Gilliatt put the parcel carefully into the bag she was carrying, then said to Mr. Satterthwaite:

"Well, see you presently. Tea isn't until quarter past five, so don't worry. I'm so pleased to meet you at last, having heard so much about you always, both from Simon and from my father-in-law."

She said a hurried good-bye to Mr. Quin and went out of the shop.

"Bit of a hurry she's in, isn't she?" said the shop woman, "but she's always like that. Gets through a lot in a day, I'd say."

The sound of the motor bicycle outside was heard as it revved up.

"Quite a character, isn't she?" said Mr. Satterthwaite.

"It would seem so," said Mr. Quin.

"And I really can't persuade you?"

"I'm only passing by," said Mr. Quin.

"And when shall I see you again? I wonder now."

"Oh, it will not be very long," said Mr. Quin. "I think you will recognize me when you do see me."

"Have you nothing more — nothing more to tell me? Nothing more to explain?"

"To explain what?"

"To explain why I have met you here."

"You are a man of considerable knowledge," said Mr. Quin. "One word might mean something to you. I think it would and it might come in useful."

"What word?"

"Daltonism," said Mr. Quin. He smiled.

"I don't think —" Mr. Satterthwaite frowned for a moment. "Yes. Yes, I do know, only just for the moment I can't remember. . . ."

"Good-bye for the present," said Mr.

Quin. "Here is your car."

At that moment the car was indeed pulling up by the post office door. Mr. Satterthwaite went out to it. He was anxious not to waste more time and keep his hosts waiting longer than need be. But he was sad all the same at saying good-bye to his friend.

"There is nothing I can do for you?" he said, and his tone was almost wistful.

"Nothing you can do for *me*."

"For someone else?"

"I think so. Very likely."

"I hope I know what you mean."

"I have the utmost faith in you," said Mr. Quin. "You always know things. You are very quick to observe and to know the meaning of things. You have not changed, I assure you."

His hand rested for a moment on Mr. Satterthwaite's shoulder, then he walked out and proceeded briskly down the village street in the opposite direction to Doverton Kingsbourne. Mr. Satterthwaite got into his car.

"I hope we shan't have any more trouble," he said.

His chauffeur reassured him.

"It's no distance from here, sir. Three or four miles at most, and she's running beautifully now."

He ran the car a little way along the street

and turned where the road widened so as to return the way he had just come. He said again,

"Only three or four miles."

Mr. Satterthwaite said again, "Daltonism." It still didn't mean anything to him, but yet he felt it should. It was a word he'd heard used before.

"Doverton Kingsbourne," said Mr. Satterthwaite to himself. He said it very softly under his breath. The two words still meant to him what they had always meant. A place of joyous reunion, a place where he couldn't get there too quickly. A place where he was going to enjoy himself, even though so many of those whom he had known would not be there any longer. But Tom would be there. His old friend Tom, and he thought again of the grass and the lake and the river and the things they had done together as boys.

Tea was set out upon the lawn. Steps led out from the French windows in the drawing room and down to where a big copper beech at one side and a cedar of Lebanon on the other made the setting for the afternoon scene. There were two painted and carved white tables and various garden chairs. Upright ones with colored cushions, and lounging ones where you could lean back and stretch your feet out and sleep, if you wished to do so. Some of them had hoods over them to guard you from the sun.

It was a beautiful early evening and the green of the grass was a soft deep color. The golden light came through the copper beech and the cedar showed the lines of its beauty against a soft pinkish-golden sky.

Tom Addison was waiting for his guest in a long basket chair, his feet up. Mr. Satterthwaite noted with some amusement what he remembered from many other occasions of meeting his host — he had comfortable bedroom slippers suited to his slightly swollen gouty feet, and the shoes were odd ones. One red and one green. Good old Tom, thought Mr. Satterthwaite, he hasn't changed. Just the same. And he thought, "What an idiot I am. Of course I know what the word meant. Why didn't I think of it at once?"

"Thought you were never going to turn up, you old devil," said Tom Addison.

He was still a handsome old man, a broad face with deepset twinkling grey eyes, shoulders that were still square and gave him a look of power. Every line in his face seemed a line of good humor and affectionate welcome. "He never changes," thought Mr. Satterthwaite.

"Can't get up to greet you," said Tom Addison. "Takes two strong men and a stick to get me on my feet. Now, do you know our little crowd, or don't you? You know Simon, of course."

"Of course I do. It's a good few years since I've seen you, but you haven't changed much."

Squadron Leader Simon Gilliatt was a lean, handsome man with a mop of red hair.

"Sorry you never came to see us when we were in Kenya," he said. "You'd have enjoyed yourself. Lots of things we could have shown you. Ah well, one can't see what the future may bring. I thought I'd lay my bones in that country."

"We've got a very nice churchyard here," said Tom Addison. "Nobody's ruined our church yet by restoring it and we haven't very much new building round about so there's plenty of room in the churchyard still. We haven't had one of these terrible additions of a new intake of graves."

"What a gloomy conversation you're having," said Beryl Gilliatt, smiling. "These are our boys," she said, "but you know them already, don't you, Mr. Satterthwaite?"

"I don't think I'd have known them now," said Mr. Satterthwaite.

Indeed, the last time he had seen the two

boys was on a day when he had taken them out from their prep school. Although there was no relationship between them — they had different fathers and mothers — the boys could have been, and often were, taken for brothers. They were about the same height and they both had red hair. Roland, presumably, having inherited it from his father and Timothy from his auburn-haired another. There seemed also to be a kind of comradeship between them. Yet really, Mr. Satterthwaite thought, they were very different. The difference was clearer now when they were, he supposed, between twenty-two and twenty-five years old. He could see no resemblance in Roland to his grandfather. Nor apart from his red hair did he look like his father.

Mr. Satterthwaite had wondered sometimes whether the boy would look like Lily, his dead mother. But there again he could see little resemblance. If anything, Timothy looked more as a son of Lily's might have looked. The fair skin and the high forehead and a delicacy of bone structure. At his elbow, a soft deep voice said,

"I'm Inez. I don't expect you remember me. It was quite a long time ago when I saw you."

A beautiful girl, Mr. Satterthwaite thought

at once. A dark type. He cast his mind back a long way to the days when he had come to be best man at Tom Addison's wedding to Pilar. She showed her Spanish blood, he thought, the carriage of her head and the dark aristocratic beauty. Her father, Dr. Horton, was standing just behind her. He looked much older than when Mr. Satterthwaite had seen him last. A nice man and kindly. A good general practitioner, unambitious but reliable and devoted, Mr. Satterthwaite thought, to his daughter. He was obviously immensely proud of her.

Mr. Satterthwaite felt an enormous happiness creeping over him. All these people, he thought, although some of them strange to him, seemed like friends he had already known. The dark beautiful girl, the two red-haired boys, Beryl Gilliatt, fussing over the tea tray, arranging cups and saucers, beckoning to a maid from the house to bring out cakes and plates of sandwiches. A splendid tea. There were chairs that pulled up to the tables so that you could sit comfortably eating all you wanted to eat. The boys settled themselves, inviting Mr. Satterthwaite to sit between them.

He was pleased at that. He had already planned in his own mind that it was the boys he wanted to talk to first, to see how much they recalled to him Tom Addison in the old days, and he thought, "Lily. How I wish Lily could be here now." Here he was, thought Mr. Satterthwaite, here he was back in his boyhood. Here where he had come and been welcomed by Tom's father and mother, an aunt or so, too, there had been, and a great-uncle and cousins. And now, well, there were not so many in this family, but it *was* a family. Tom in his bedroom slippers, one red, one green, old but still merry and happy. Happy in those who were spread round him. And here was Doverton just, or almost just, as it had been. Not quite so well kept up, perhaps, but the lawn was in good condition. And down there he could see the gleam of the river through the trees and the trees, too. More trees than there had been. And the house needing, perhaps, another coat of paint but not too badly. After all, Tom Addison was a rich man. Well provided for, owning a large quantity of land. A man with simple tastes who spent enough to keep his place up but was not a spendthrift in other ways. He seldom traveled or went abroad nowadays, but he entertained. Not big parties, just friends. Friends who came to stay, friends who usually had some connections going back into the past. A friendly house.

He turned a little in his chair, drawing it

away from the table and turning it sideways so that he could see better the view down to the river. Down there was the mill, of course, and beyond the other side there were fields. And in one of the fields, it amused him to see a kind of scarecrow, a dark figure on which birds were settling on the straw. Just for a moment he thought it looked like Mr. Harley Quin. Perhaps, thought Mr. Satterthwaite, it *is* my friend Mr. Quin. It was an absurd idea, and yet if someone had piled up the scarecrow and tried to make it look like Mr. Quin, it could have had the sort of slender elegance that was foreign to most scarecrows one saw.

"Are you looking at our scarecrow?" said Timothy. "We've got a name for him, you know. We call him Mister Harley Barley."

"Do you indeed," said Mr. Satterthwaite. "Dear me, I find that very interesting."

"Why do you find it interesting?" said Roly, with some curiosity.

"Well, because it rather resembles someone that I know, whose name happens to be Harley. His first name, that is."

The boys began singing, *"Harley Barley, stands on guard, Harley Barley takes things hard. Guards the ricks and guards the hay, Keeps the trespassers away."*

"Cucumber sandwich, Mr. Satterthwaite?" said Beryl Gilliatt, "or do you prefer a home-made pâté one?"

Mr. Satterthwaite accepted the home-made pâté. She deposited by his side a puce cup, the same color as he had admired in the shop. How gay it looked, all that tea set on the table. Yellow, red, blue, green, and all the rest of it. He wondered if each one had his favorite color. Timothy, he noticed, had a red cup, Roland had a yellow one. Beside Timothy's cup was an object Mr. Satterthwaite could not at first identify. Then he saw it was a meerschaum pipe. It was years since Mr. Satterthwaite had thought of or seen a meerschaum pipe. Roland, noticing what he was looking at, said, "Tim brought that back from Germany when he went. He's killing himself with cancer smoking his pipe all the time."

"Don't you smoke, Roland?"

"No. I'm not one for smoking. I don't smoke cigarettes and I don't smoke pot either."

Inez came to the table and sat down on the other side of him. Both the young men pressed food upon her. They started a laughing conversation together.

Mr. Satterthwaite felt very happy among these young people. Not that they took very much notice of him apart from their natural politeness. But he liked hearing them. He liked, too, making up his judgement about them. He thought, he was almost sure, that both the young men were in love with Inez. Well, it was not surprising. Propinquity brings these things about. They had come to live here with their grandfather. A beautiful girl, Roland's first cousin, was living almost next door. Mr. Satterthwaite turned his head. He could just see the house through the trees where it poked up from the road just beyond the front gate. That was the same house that Dr. Horton had lived in last time he came here, seven or eight years ago.

He looked at Inez. He wondered which of the two young men she preferred or whether her affections were already engaged elsewhere. There was no reason why she should not fall in love with one of these two attractive young specimens of the male race.

Having eaten as much as he wanted — it was not very much — Mr. Satterthwaite drew his chair back, altering its angle a little so that he could look all round him.

Mrs. Gilliatt was still busy. Very much the housewife, he thought, making perhaps rather more of a fuss than she need of domesticity. Continually offering people cakes, taking their cups away and replenishing them, handing things round. Somehow, he thought, it would be more pleasant and more informal if she let people help themselves. He wished she was not so busy a hostess.

He looked up to the place where Tom Addison lay stretched out in his chair. Tom Addison was also watching Beryl Gilliatt. Mr. Satterthwaite thought to himself: "He doesn't like her. No. Tom doesn't like her. Well, perhaps that's to be expected." After all, Beryl had taken the place of his own daughter, of Simon Gilliatt's first wife, Lily. "My beautiful Lily," thought Mr. Satterthwaite again, and wondered why for some reason he felt that although he could not see anyone like her, Lily in some strange way was here. She was here at this tea party.

"I suppose one begins to imagine these things as one gets old," said Mr. Satterthwaite to himself. "After all, why shouldn't Lily be here to see her son."

He looked affectionately at Timothy and then suddenly realized that he was not looking at Lily's son. Roland was Lily's son. Timothy was Beryl's son.

"I believe Lily knows I'm here. I believe she'd like to speak to me," said Mr. Satterthwaite. "Oh dear, oh dear, I mustn't start imagining foolish things."

For some reason he looked again at the scarecrow. It didn't look like a scarecrow now. It looked like Mr. Harley Quin. Some tricks of the light, of the sunset, were providing it with color, and there was a black dog like Hermes chasing the birds.

"Color," said Mr. Satterthwaite, and looked again at the table and the tea set and the people having tea. "Why am I here?" said Mr. Satterthwaite. "Why am I here and what ought I to be doing? There's a reason. . . ."

Now he knew, he felt, there was something, some crisis, something affecting — affecting all these people or only some of them? Beryl Gilliatt, Mrs. Gilliatt. She was nervous about something. On edge. Tom? Nothing wrong with Tom. He wasn't affected. A lucky man to own this beauty, to own Doverton and to have a grandson so that when he died all this would come to Roland. All this would be Roland's. Was Tom hoping that Roland would marry Inez? Or would he have a fear of first cousins marrying? Though throughout history, Mr. Satterthwaite thought, brothers had married sisters with no ill result. "Nothing must happen," said Mr. Satterthwaite, "nothing must happen. I must prevent it."

Really, his thoughts were the thoughts of a madman. A peaceful scene. A tea set. The varying colors of the Harlequin cups. He looked at the white meerschaum pipe lying against the red of the cup. Beryl Gilliatt said something to Timothy. Timothy nodded, got up and went off towards the house. Beryl removed some empty plates from the table, adjusted a chair or two, murmured something to Roland, who went across and offered a frosted cake to Dr. Horton.

Mr. Satterthwaite watched her. He had to watch her. The sweep of her sleeve as she passed the table. He saw a red cup get pushed off the table. It broke on the iron feet of a chair. He heard her little exclamation as she picked up the bits. She went to the tea tray, came back and placed on the table a pale blue cup and saucer. She replaced the meerschaum pipe, putting it close against it. She brought the teapot and poured tea, then she moved away.

The table was untenanted now. Inez also had got up and left it. Gone to speak to her grandfather. "I don't understand," said Mr. Satterthwaite to himself. "Something's going to happen. What's going to happen?"

A table with different-colored cups round, and — yes, Timothy, his red hair glowing in the sun. Red hair glowing with that same tint, that attractive sideways wave that Simon Gilliatt's hair had always had. Timothy, coming back, standing a moment, looking at the table with a slightly puzzled eye, then going to where the meerschaum pipe rested against the pale blue cup.

Inez came back then. She laughed suddenly and she said, "Timothy, you're drinking your tea out of the wrong cup. The blue cup's mine. Yours is the red one."

And Timothy said, "Don't be silly, Inez, I know my own cup. It's got sugar in it and you won't like it. Nonsense. This is my cup. The meerschaum's up against it."

It came to Mr. Satterthwaite then. A shock. Was he mad? Was he imagining things? Was any of this real?

He got up. He walked quickly towards the table, and as Timothy raised the blue cup to his lips, he shouted.

"Don't drink that!" he called. "Don't drink it, I say."

Timothy turned a surprised face. Mr. Satterthwaite turned his head. Dr. Horton, rather startled, got up from his seat and was coming near.

"What's the matter, Satterthwaite?"

"That cup. There's something wrong about it," said Mr. Satterthwaite. "Don't let the boy drink from it."

Horton stared at it. "My dear fellow —"

"I know what I'm saying. The red cup was his," said Mr. Satterthwaite, "and the red cup's broken. It's been replaced with a blue one. He doesn't know the red from blue, does he?"

Dr. Horton looked puzzled. "D'you mean — d'you mean — like Tom?"

"Tom Addison. He's color-blind. You know that, don't you?"

"Oh yes, of course. We all know that. That's why he'd got odd shoes on today. He never knew red from green."

"This boy is the same."

"But — but surely not. Anyway, there's never been any sign of it in — in Roland."

"There might be, though, mightn't there?" said Mr. Satterthwaite. "I'm right in thinking — Daltonism. That's what they call it, don't they?"

"It was a name they used to call it by, yes."

"It's not inherited by a female, but it passes through the female. Lily wasn't color-blind, but Lily's son might easily be color-blind."

"But my dear Satterthwaite, Timothy isn't Lily's son. Roly is Lily's son. I know they're rather alike. Same age, same-colored hair and things, but — well, perhaps you don't remember."

"No," said Mr. Satterthwaite, "I shouldn't have remembered. But I know now. I can see the resemblance too. Roland's Beryl's son. They were both babies, weren't they,

293

when Simon remarried. It is very easy for a woman looking after two babies, especially if both of them were going to have red hair. Timothy's Lily's son and Roland is Beryl's son. Beryl's and Christopher Eden's. There is no reason why he should be color-blind. I know it, I tell you. I know it!"

He saw Dr. Horton's eyes go from one to the other. Timothy, not catching what they said but standing holding the blue cup and looking puzzled.

"I saw her buy it," said Mr. Satterthwaite. "Listen to me, man. You must listen to me. You've known me for some years. You know that I don't make mistakes if I say a thing positively."

"Quite true. I've never known you to make a mistake."

"Take that cup away from him," said Mr. Satterthwaite. "Take it back to your surgery or take it to an analytic chemist and find out what's in it. I saw that woman buy that cup. She bought it in the village shop. She knew then that she was going to break a red cup, replace it by a blue and that Timothy would never know that the colors were different."

"I think you're mad, Satterthwaite. But all the same I'm going to do what you say."

He advanced on the table, stretched out a hand to the blue cup.

"Do you mind letting me have a look at that?" said Dr. Horton.

"Of course," said Timothy. He looked slightly surprised.

"I think there's a flaw in the china, here, you know. Rather interesting."

Beryl came across the lawn. She came quickly and sharply.

"What are you doing? What's the matter? What is happening?"

"Nothing's the matter," said Dr. Horton, cheerfully. "I just want to show the boys a little experiment I'm going to make with a cup of tea."

He was looking at her very closely and he saw the expression of fear, of terror. Mr. Satterthwaite saw the entire change of countenance.

"Would you like to come with me, Satterthwaite? Just a little experiment, you know. A matter of testing porcelain and different qualities in it nowadays. A very interesting discovery was made lately."

Chatting, he walked along the grass. Mr. Satterthwaite followed him and the two young men, chatting to each other, followed him.

"What's the Doc up to now, Roly?" said Timothy.

"I don't know," said Roland. "He seems

to have got some very extraordinary ideas. Oh well, we shall hear about it later, I expect. Let's go and get our bikes."

Beryl Gilliatt turned abruptly. She retraced her steps rapidly up the lawn towards the house. Tom Addison called to her:

"Anything the matter, Beryl?"

"Something I'd forgotten," said Beryl Gilliatt. "That's all."

Tom Addison looked inquiringly towards Simon Gilliatt.

"Anything wrong with your wife?" he said.

"Beryl? Oh no, not that I know of. I expect it's some little thing or other that she's forgotten. Nothing I can do for you, Beryl?" he called.

"No. No, I'll be back later." She turned her head half sideways, looking at the old man lying back in the chair. She spoke suddenly and vehemently. "You silly old fool. You've got the wrong shoes on again today. They don't match. Do you know you've got one shoe that's red and one shoe that's green?"

"Ah, done it again, have I?" said Tom Addison. "They look exactly the same color to me, you know. It's odd, isn't it, but there it is."

She went past him, her steps quickening. Presently Mr. Satterthwaite and Dr. Horton reached the gate that led out into the roadway. They heard a motor bicycle speeding along.

"She's gone," said Dr. Horton. "She's run for it. We ought to have stopped her, I suppose. Do you think she'll come back?"

"No," said Mr. Satterthwaite, "I don't think she'll come back. Perhaps," he said thoughtfully, "it's best left that way."

"You mean?"

"It's an old house," said Mr. Satterthwaite. "And an old family. A good family. A lot of good people in it. One doesn't want trouble, scandal, everything brought upon it. Best to let her go, I think."

"Tom Addison never liked her," said Dr. Horton. "Never. He was always polite and kind but he didn't like her."

"And there's the boy to think of," said Mr. Satterthwaite.

"The boy. You mean?"

"The other boy. Roland. This way he needn't know about what his mother was trying to do."

"Why did she do it? Why on earth did she do it?"

"You've no doubt now that she did," said Mr. Satterthwaite.

"No. I've no doubt now. I saw her face, Satterthwaite, when she looked at me. I knew then that what you'd said was truth. But why?"

"Greed, I suppose," said Mr. Satterthwaite. "She hadn't any money of her own, I believe. Her husband, Christopher Eden, was a nice chap by all accounts but he hadn't anything in the way of means. But Tom Addison's grandchild has got big money coming to him. A lot of money. Property all around here has appreciated enormously. I've no doubt that Tom Addison will leave the bulk of what he has to his grandson. She wanted it for her own son and through her own son, of course, for herself. She is a greedy woman."

Mr. Satterthwaite turned his head back suddenly.

"Something's on fire over there," he said.

"Good lord, so it is. Oh, it's the scarecrow down in the field. Some young chap or other's set fire to it, I suppose. But there's nothing to worry about. There are no ricks or anything anywhere near. It'll just burn itself out."

"Yes," said Mr. Satterthwaite. "Well, you go on, Doctor. You don't need me to help you in your tests."

"I've no doubt of what I shall find. I don't mean the exact substance, but I have come to your belief that this blue cup holds death."

Mr. Satterthwaite had turned back

through the gate. He was going now down in the direction where the scarecrow was burning. Behind it was the sunset. A remarkable sunset that evening. Its colors illuminated the air round it, illuminated the burning scarecrow.

"So that's the way you've chosen to go," said Mr. Satterthwaite.

He looked slightly startled then, for in the neighborhood of the flames he saw the tall, slight figure of a woman. A woman dressed in some pale mother-of-pearl coloring. She was walking in the direction of Mr. Satterthwaite. He stopped dead, watching.

"Lily," he said. "Lily."

He saw her quite plainly now. It was Lily walking towards him. Too far away for him to see her face but he knew very well who it was. Just for a moment or two he wondered whether anyone else would see her or whether the sight was only for him. He said, not very loud, only in a whisper,

"It's all right, Lily, your son is safe."

She stopped then. She raised one hand to her lips. He didn't see her smile, but he knew she was smiling. She kissed her hand and waved it to him and then she turned. She walked back towards where the scarecrow was disintegrating into a mass of ashes.

"She's going away again," said Mr. Satterthwaite to himself. "She's going away with him. They're walking away together. They belong to the same world, of course. They only come — those sort of people — they only come when it's a case of love or death or both."

He wouldn't see Lily again, he supposed, but he wondered how soon he would meet Mr. Quin again. He turned then and went back across the lawn towards the tea table and the Harlequin tea set, and beyond that, to his old friend Tom Addison. Beryl wouldn't come back. He was sure of it. Doverton Kingsbourne was safe again.

Across the lawn came the small black dog in flying leaps. It came to Mr. Satterthwaite, panting a little and wagging its tail. Through its collar was twisted a scrap of paper. Mr. Satterthwaite stooped and detached it — smoothing it out — on it in colored letters was written a message:

Congratulations! To Our Next Meeting

H. Q.

"Thank you, Hermes," said Mr. Satterthwaite, and watched the black dog flying across the meadow to rejoin the two figures that he himself knew were there but could no longer see.

300

We hope you have enjoyed this Large Print book. Other Thorndike Press or Chivers Press Large Print books are available at your library or directly from the publishers.

For more information about current and upcoming titles, please call or write, without obligation, to:

Thorndike Press
P.O. Box 159
Thorndike, Maine 04986 USA
Tel. (800) 257-5157

OR

Chivers Press Limited
Windsor Bridge Road
Bath BA2 3AX
England
Tel. (0225) 335336

All our Large Print titles are designed for easy reading, and all our books are made to last.